Praise for *School*

'Jesse is the fr...
He'll get you into trouble, he'll get you out
of it and he'll be standing right next
to you in the principal's office.
Prepare yourself for a rollicking ride!'

NAT AMOORE

author of *Secrets of a Schoolyard Millionaire*

'A hilarious, heartfelt book that made me
laugh, cringe and gasp, sometimes all at
the same time. It's a full-on fun fest!'

OLIVER PHOMMAVANH

author of *Thai-riffic!*

'Hilarious hijinks abound! A must-read for
any kid who's ever lost their school jumper
or had their belongings eaten by a goat.'

KATE and JOL TEMPLE

authors of *Yours Troolie, Alice Toolie*

'A super funny, highly witty and fantastically authentic look at Grade 6 life in Australia ... Screams fun and authenticity and holds its own against Diary of a Wimpy Kid, Tom Gates and Timmy Failure.'

READING TIME

'Full of surprises and action. Make sure you read to the end because the last two chapters are the best! I rate this book five stars.'

DANIEL, AGE 9

KIDS' READING GUIDE

THE GRADE 6 SURVIVAL GUIDE

A CLASS FULL OF LIZARDS

ALISON HART

ALLEN&UNWIN
SYDNEY • MELBOURNE • AUCKLAND • LONDON

First published by Allen & Unwin in 2021

Allen & Unwin
83 Alexander Street
Crows Nest NSW 2065
Australia
Phone: (61 2) 8425 0100
Email: info@allenandunwin.com
Web: www.allenandunwin.com

A catalogue record for this
book is available from the
National Library of Australia

ISBN 978 1 76087 737 8

For teaching resources, explore www.allenandunwin.com/resources/for-teachers

Cover illustration by Liz Anelli
Cover and text design by Mika Tabata
Set in 13 pt Crimson Text by Midland Typesetters, Australia
This book was printed in January 2021 by McPherson's Printing Group, Australia

10 9 8 7 6 5 4 3 2 1

The paper in this book is FSC® certified.
FSC® promotes environmentally responsible,
socially beneficial and economically viable
management of the world's forests.

For Mum

CHAPTER ONE

The first bell is already ringing as I walk through the front gate of Westmoore Primary. I know it's the first bell and not the second bell because everyone in the playground is ignoring it.

I nearly didn't make it to school on time because I waited *ten* whole minutes on the corner for Braden. He only lives four houses away from me so we usually walk to school together. But he didn't show up today.

His face appears through an open window in the corridor.

'Hey, Jesse!' he yells. 'I just remembered we were supposed to walk to school together!'

'I know. I waited for ages,' I say.

'How long?'

'*Half an hour,*' I say and laugh when his eyes go wide.

'Sorry! I forgot …'

'Ha-ha … just kidding. But didn't you go right past my house?'

'I did,' Braden says, 'but I was in the car. Dad dropped me off at school at eight o'clock.'

Eight o'clock! It's a good thing he didn't come into our house at eight o'clock. I was still in my pyjamas.

Braden's freckled face disappears back through the window.

There are no kids blocking the main steps to the corridor, which is good because I don't feel like taking the long way around. Inside, books and socks and half-eaten lunches are flying all over the place. Most of the kids from my Grade 6 class are standing in a nervous cluster outside our classroom. We can't put our stuff away because our teacher Mrs Leeman keeps the door locked before and after school, during recess *and* at lunchtime.

Our access is restricted to the six dreary hours we already have in there.

My friend Jun and a couple of other kids are staring at something on Minha's mobile phone. Minha is in my class and Mrs Leeman will be here in about two minutes' time. What could be so interesting that she has her phone out *now*?

'Have a look at this,' Jun says when he sees me. '*Fish.*'

The picture is blurry, but I can see three little goldfish crowded around some miniature plastic trees stuck in coloured gravel. Ordinary goldfish. They're not interesting at all. I'm about to look away when one of them moves.

'It's a video?' I ask.

'Yeah, *look*,' Jun says again.

The camera follows the goldfish along the tank, past more trees, a treasure chest and a sunken hotel. There's more furniture in the tank than we have in our whole house. Right at the other end, in front of a ruined castle, there's another fish about five times as big as the goldfish. He's massive. He's got big, boggly eyes the size of peas stuck on each side of his head.

The other fish reach the castle, then turn around and start swimming back again. The boggly-eyed one doesn't need to swim around because he can see in every direction at the same time without moving. Mrs Leeman can see in every direction with normal eyes, which is why Minha should put her phone away.

Otherwise it will be the first confiscated item of Term 3.

The second bell goes. There's no sign of my best friend Alex.

It's weird because he's never late.

Mrs Leeman arrives at 9.01 am and we shuffle over a bit to let her through. She takes out a big bunch of keys and unlocks our classroom as if on the other side of the door it's the land of chocolate and not the sand bunker of boredom. For a minute I think we're in the wrong room because everything looks different. Posters on the walls about stuff we did *last* term have been replaced with maps and graphs about population density and stuff. None of us know where to sit because the desks have been moved around. Now they're arranged in two big blocks facing the front with an aisle down the middle. Like a movie theatre except it's all one level and there's nothing interesting going on up the front. We're instructed to find the desk with our name on it. Mine is on the aisle. I'm totally exposed on the right. Mrs Leeman can see what I'm doing at all times.

Class begins without any discussion about anything. A diagram of overlapping triangles appears on the interactive whiteboard. As we start a boring lesson *about* the triangles, I have a quick look around the room. There are two empty desks: one up the front, and another up the back. Jun and Braden are sitting as far from me as possible while still being in the room. In fact, as I look around, I notice *everyone* has been separated from their friends. Mrs Leeman must have some kind of social network informant. No one is sitting anywhere near close enough to pass anything to or talk with their friends. Mrs Leeman would be really good at those games where you have to keep some things away from other things, so they don't get eaten or die.

About ten minutes into the lesson, Ian, the student teacher from last term, knocks on the square bit of window in our classroom door. Everyone jumps because Mrs Leeman insists on total silence unless she is speaking. We're too scared even to unzip our pencil cases. He opens the door a little bit and sticks his head around. I notice his hair is short now; the ponytail is gone. I wonder if he still has it somewhere. My nanna's still got her old hair in a yellow envelope from forty-two years ago.

Ian says, 'Hey, guys! Hi, Mrs Leeman! Sorry to interrupt. I was wondering if I could borrow Jesse for a tic?'

Mrs Leeman peers over her wiry glasses and says I can leave as long as I'm not away from class for too long. How do *I* know how long I'm going to be? I don't even know why I'm going. I don't even know *where* I'm going or why Ian is the one to take me.

I can feel everyone looking at me as I walk up the aisle towards the door. I follow Ian up to the administration building.

'I thought Alex might like a bit of moral support,' he says, mysteriously. He marches straight up to Mr Wilson's office and knocks on the door.

When we open the door, I'm only expecting to see Mr Wilson and maybe Alex, but the vice-principal's office is full of people. Alex is there and so are his parents. There's also a bearded guy with a hairy green jumper. Everyone stops talking and stares at us.

Hairy-Green-Jumper guy says, 'Jesse! Jesse? Tell me! Have you and Alex been friends for long?'

He must be one of those people who asks you a question when they already know the answer. Maybe it's a trick question.

I'm just thinking about how to answer it when he asks, 'So! Do you think Alex could be bored in Mrs Leeman's class?'

Now I *know* it's a trick. We are *all* bored in Mrs Leeman's class. If I was on TV, I would ask for a lawyer.

Ian leans forwards. 'Don't stress, Jesse. Alex will put you in the picture. We're just tossing around some ideas today.'

Mr Wilson announces to the room in general: 'Ian is our Wellbeing Officer.'

Ian's a *Wellbeing Officer* now? He didn't last very long as a teacher.

I have no idea what's going on. It's not until we're walking back to class that Alex explains what the meeting was all about.

'I might be going to St Brainiac's next year,' he says. '*Might* be … they've offered me a scholarship.'

St Brainiac's is really St Bennett's college. It *sounds* like a boarding school from two hundred years ago and it looks like one too. I know because we've driven past it a few times. The building is really old and there's a big, high wall all the way around it. It's only for really smart kids, so there's no chance I'll be offered a place as well. 'I have to go every Wednesday to see if I like it better than here,' Alex says.

He says the guy with the hairy green jumper in

Mr Wilson's office is the principal! I can't believe it. He looked like he'd just wandered in from taking his dog for a walk.

The school costs a lot of money, which doesn't make sense because the kids are already smart. They should put the money towards kids who have a workbook full of impossible maths questions and feel like burying it.

As we walk up the steps to the corridor, I say to Alex, 'Have you ever noticed Ian speaks like the phrase-a-day calendar on Mrs Leeman's desk? *Let me put you in the picture … I'm just tossing around ideas.*'

Alex starts laughing. 'Yeah. I have to see Ian about going to St Bennett's. He says he wants to *talk it over with me.*'

'I hope he *goes out on a limb for you,*' I say, and we both crack up.

We have to stop laughing before we reach class though because Mrs Leeman has no sense of humour and will ask, 'what's so funny?' and make us repeat it to the class. I don't say anything to Alex, but I secretly hope that St Bennett's has made a mistake and they don't have a spot for him after all. I just assumed we would go to the *same* school next year. I don't want to go by myself.

The triangles are off the board when we get into the classroom. I head back to my centre-aisle desk and Alex finds his desk right up the back. I can't even see him from where I'm sitting.

Mrs Leeman says we are going to study 'our closest neighbours'. She wants us to choose one neighbour and make a wall poster with a map, using proper information – at least three references.

Mr Mancini is my closest neighbour. I hope he doesn't mind being the subject of a wall poster. The information will have to be accurate because Mr Mancini and Mrs Leeman might know each other. He is really old, too. The map will be easy. I'll just put our street in the middle. I know he goes to the supermarket every morning and the Italian club every Friday night. I don't know about references, but I can ask him about the other stuff.

Mrs Leeman says this is a homework assignment and that we're not allowed to work together. I don't know who Alex will write about. He has a footy oval on one side and a mean old lady on the other who throws all her compost over the fence and into their swimming pool.

When the bell rings for recess, all the kids from the other grades pour into the corridor, but we're not allowed to move until Mrs Leeman says so. Our friend Peta from the other Grade 6 class peers in through the window of our classroom door. I wish she wouldn't do that. It looks really funny, but smiling is frowned upon in our class and laughing is totally off limits.

When we are eventually let out, Alex, Braden, Jun and I find Peta still waiting in the corridor.

'Where were you all holidays?' Braden asks her.

'The first week I didn't do much, but the second week I went to stay with my brother,' Peta says. 'He has an emu farm.'

An *emu* farm? I didn't know there was such a thing. Emus give me the creeps. I hate the clonking sound they make and the way they step onto the bus if you're on a school excursion.

'Yeah, he's got six hundred emus,' Peta continues, 'and after their eggs hatch we—'

'How big are they?' Jun interrupts. 'The eggs, I mean.'

Peta holds her hands out to show us. It's about half the size of a football, only egg-shaped.

'Then what?' I ask.

'After their eggs hatch, people come to look at the chicks. We only let people hold them if they sit still, and don't hold them too tight.'

'What if they don't want to hold them?' Braden says.

'They don't *have* to hold them.' Peta giggles. 'Most people just look at the chicks and buy stuff from the gift shop. We have emu oil, emu soap, emu candles and emu steaks.'

That would give me the creeps if I was an emu.

I stayed home all holidays because Dad said we're spending our holiday money on a new roof because the one we have is full of holes. I don't remember that discussion. My older brother Noah went away to Central Australia with his school, so that must not count. It was okay though because Alex and I had the house to ourselves. I always prefer it when Alex comes over to my place rather than the other way around. His house has no mess anywhere and you have to leave your shoes at the door. At our place we never take our shoes off and nobody vacuums until the dog hair is rolling around in balls all over the floor.

Instead of going straight down to the water tanks like we usually do, we have a bit of a look around the school. There's been a few changes since last term. The adventure playground has been replaced and the new toilet block is nearly finished. The ground where they had to replace the pipe after it exploded is taped off so kids don't run on the new grass seed. At the moment there's about five hundred pigeons eating it. Every time someone goes near it, the pigeons fly about twenty centimetres in the air then land again and keep eating.

Peta tells us we didn't have assembly this morning because our principal, Mrs Overbeek, isn't coming back to school until Wednesday. Her teacher, Ms Kendall, keeps their class updated about everything that's going on. Mrs Leeman doesn't tell us anything until we are about to do it or are already doing it. I hadn't even thought about assembly until then. How can Mrs Overbeek not come back until Wednesday? I'd like to go on holiday and not come back until I felt like it. I would never come back. Also, Mrs Overbeek should be concerned that school is running perfectly well without her.

She obviously doesn't do anything important.

We don't get time to look at the new adventure playground because the bell rings. We weren't going to play on it or anything, we just wanted to see what it's like. It's not fair we had to put up with the old one that was falling apart for years and now the school gets a new one when we're in Grade 6 and too old to use it.

Back in class, we all take our seats in the movie theatre. I've figured out I can see Alex if I turn right around or bend down to pick something up off the floor. A couple of times, I turn my head upside down to catch his eye, but Mrs Leeman catches me doing it and asks me if I need to go to sick bay.

The threat of sick bay is enough to make me face the front for the rest of the lesson. Sick bay is in the office and so is Miss Creighton, the most horrible office lady in the Southern Hemisphere.

At lunchtime, the five of us – Alex, Jun, Braden, Peta and me – head down to the water tanks. There's no way we can hang out there now. It's still wet from the flood last term. The ground *looks* solid but if you step on it, your foot sinks into green slimy mud that stinks. We find a big branch about a metre long to see how far we can stick it in the ground. It disappears completely. We get a few more sticks and rocks and stuff and all of them sink under the surface. Now that I know Alex's dad is a groundwater hydrologist, I keep noticing water on and in the ground all the time. He would probably find this whole area cool and interesting and want to write a fifty-page report about it.

I'm happy when the others say they've had enough, because the smell is making me feel sick. Also, there are about a *billion* mosquitos.

Eventually we decide to relocate to the retaining wall opposite the classrooms. It's not a perfect lunch spot but then, we're at school – we need to keep our expectations realistic. We *are* a bit exposed, though. Everyone can see us. After about five minutes, Thomas Moore, my Prep buddy, comes running over to us even though we haven't had anything to do with our buddies since Term 2.

'What are we doing today?' he asks me.

'*We* are not doing anything,' I reply. '*You* have to play with the other Preps now.'

'None of them will play with me.'

'Oh. Maybe ask your teacher what to do?' I tell him.

'I did. Miss Agostino said to come and find *you*.'

'You'll be bored here with us,' Alex tells him. 'We don't play around or anything.'

'I don't mind,' Thomas Moore says.

'You can stay for today,' Peta says, walking over, 'until you find some friends.'

'Yeah,' Braden says, 'but don't bring all the Preps over here. This is our spot. Okay?'

Thomas Moore climbs up on the end of the wall.

'This is our spot,' he repeats, nodding.

In the afternoon, before we go home, Mrs Leeman says Minha has something she wants to share with the class. Minha stands up but she doesn't walk to the front so we all have to turn around and find where the voice is coming from. Her desk is down the back, next to Alex's.

'Okay, yeah. We have some fish at the rescue centre at the moment that need a home,' Minha says. 'So, if anyone wants some fish, we've got some. They come with the tank and filter and everything.'

I think back to the video she showed at the beginning of the day. I wouldn't mind some pet fish. I wonder if I'd be allowed to have these ones?

Minha sits back down for two seconds, and then jumps up again. 'Oh, yeah! There's four of them. The little ones are called One, Two and Three and the big one is called Bubbles.'

Bubbles?

That's not what I'm going to call it.

CHAPTER TWO

I'm glad I didn't do any work last night on the poster project because I find out the next day that when Mrs Leeman said 'our closest neighbours' she didn't mean our *actual* neighbours. She meant Australia's neighbouring *countries,* like Indonesia, Malaysia and New Zealand. Why didn't she say so? I want to say to Alex, *'Excuse me a minute. I just need to go eleven hundred kilometres next door to borrow a battery charger'* except Alex is sitting about eleven hundred kilometres away from me.

Mrs Leeman starts making her way down the aisle, writing notes on her class list of which 'neighbour' we're planning to do our project on. I think about saying Indonesia because it's one she just mentioned, but Mrs Leeman expects us to do something *like* her suggestion, not her *actual* suggestion. There's a subtle difference.

Halfway down the aisle, Mrs Leeman stops walking. She's standing at Jun's desk. He's *finished* his assignment already. It takes up his entire desk and the whole width of the aisle. At the top he's written 'My Neighbourhood – Languages of Dandelion Street'. Dandelion Street is where Jun lives with his grandparents and his dog, Tiny. On the poster the street is drawn as if from above. Each house has little coloured flags that show the nationalities of and languages spoken by the people who live inside. Lots of houses have more than one flag. At the bottom of the poster, there's a map of the world with areas coloured like the flags. He's even drawn some people and cars and stuff as well.

It makes all the maps and graphs on the walls of the classroom look even more boring than they did yesterday.

Mrs Leeman stares at the poster for a minute then picks it up and walks back to her desk. She opens the top drawer. It's a tense moment because she keeps everything in that drawer: scissors, black marker, detention book and most of our confiscated items. She takes out four Grippy Bits. Grippy Bits are for putting stuff up on the wall that's too good to get drawing pin holes in. The box in Mrs Leeman's desk looks about fifty years old.

She puts Jun's poster on the wall and returns to her desk. She says we can either do an assignment on one of our international neighbours *or* we can do what Jun has done: a map of our local neighbourhood, showing cultural diversity in an interesting way. We don't have to do flags … we can use our imagination and do little maps or show special days or celebrations that our neighbours observe. She says we have to go with an adult if we're visiting neighbours, and the project has to be poster-size, in colour and finished by Monday.

That's a lot of rules for an assignment that wasn't even her idea.

At recess, Peta's already down on the retaining wall when Jun, Alex, Braden and I get there. Ms Kendall lets her class out when the bell goes, unlike Mrs Leeman who lets us out when she feels like it. It's a good thing Peta's in the other class or someone else would take our spot on the wall. When you've relocated, it's important to keep a strong presence for a week at least, or someone else will say they were there first.

Alex is a bit quiet. I ask him if he's worried about going to St Brainiac's.

'Yeah … a little bit. I don't know what to wear,' he says.

'What do you mean?'

'There's no uniform. The kids can wear anything. The *teachers* can wear anything.'

'Like jeans?'

'Like trackies,' he says, giggling.

'What if Mrs Leeman wore trackies?' I laugh.

'Yeah,' Alex says. 'Trackies and *runners*.' And we both laugh so much we fall off the retaining wall.

Peta looks at us rolling around on the asphalt. 'What's *wrong* with you two? Mrs Leeman is okay.'

Only someone who isn't in Mrs Leeman's class would say something like that.

When we get back to the classroom after recess, Mrs Leeman finishes marking off our assignment topics next to our names on the roll.

I pick Mrs Leeman's original assignment because I think it could be some kind of test. Us being allowed to choose, I mean. Also, I don't want to spend a million years talking to everyone in my street. I pick the Philippines because I don't think anyone else has yet.

Being the first one to choose a country could be *part* of the test.

At home after school, I search the kitchen cupboard hoping to find a bit of cake or a chocolate biscuit or something but I can't find *anything*. There's never a lot to eat in there, but today there's literally *nothing*. Somebody hungry must have robbed the house and stolen all the food.

Mum sees me scrabbling around the cupboard in a panic. 'What are you doing?'

'Where is everything? I can't find anything to eat,' I say.

'There's plenty of things to eat, Jesse. Rice wheels, four-bean salad and the fruit bowl is full. You just need to look.'

That wasn't really a fair thing to say. I *did* look. And the only thing in the fruit bowl is fruit.

Over dinner, Mum announces that we are all going on a diet. No more processed foods, sugar, salt, fat or preservatives. Starting today. Without any warning.

'How do you know there isn't sugar and salt in this?' Noah asks, holding up a long, green thing with black dots on it.

'Because I bought all the ingredients fresh from the whole foods store,' Mum says, 'and I prepared it all myself. That way I know exactly what my family's eating.'

'Yeah, but your *family* don't know what they're eating,' Noah says, giggling.

'That's enough, Noah,' Dad says, sawing his green thing in half.

'Enough *what?*' Noah says, but only loudly enough for me to hear.

Noah and I look at each other and at the other things on our plates. There's some orange stuff underneath the green things and a few droopy leaves on top. Dad keeps an angry face on Noah until he and I both pick up our forks and pretend to eat something. I wouldn't say it's *yucky* – it isn't anything. It's like eating when you've got a head cold and everything tastes like foam.

Later on, I wait until Mum's busy watching something on TV and not really listening when I tell her I'm going to be looking after Minha's fish.

'What fish?' Mum asks, pausing the TV. 'For how long?'

'I'm not sure how long *exactly*,' I say. 'How long do fish usually live for?'

Mum turns her head towards the corner, where our dog, Milky, is sitting in Dad's armchair. 'Do you know anything about this, Andrew?'

I didn't know Dad was in the armchair until then. His head pops out from behind the dog.

'I think it's a great idea,' Dad says. 'It's about time he learned some responsibility.'

'Well, I don't know … It's quite a bit of work, looking after fish. You have to feed them, clean their tank and filter. And what happens if you go away?' Mum says to me.

'It's okay,' I promise. 'I can do it.'

The *going away* part isn't a problem. I like staying home. I can use the fish as a reason to stay home forever.

Mum turns back to the TV. 'Let me have a little think about it, Jesse. I need to decide whether you're ready for that sort of commitment.'

I'm not asking for a bank loan. They're *fish*. How much work can they be?

Dad says, 'We'll have a talk about it, Jesse, and come back to you. It's not something we can decide on the spot.'

I hope they decide 'yes' about the fish because I already told Minha I would take them. Her dad is bringing the tank around to our house on Friday.

In the morning, instead of our usual Choco-Flakes, Rice Pops and Weet Treats on the table, there are three plastic containers with varying shades of brown flakes and a container of almond milk. I'm starving so I pick the light-brown flakes and put some of the low-fat, organic almond milk on them. It's like eating wet newspaper.

I refuse Mum's offer of toast because I see what Noah has on his plate. It looks like particle board. Anyway, there's already something on my plate. It's bright red and about the size and shape of a submarine. I don't know what it is or how it got there.

Dad comes in and chooses the medium-brown flakes and puts two pieces of particle board in the toaster. There's something pink and watery in his cup instead of coffee.

'What's this thing on my plate?' I ask Mum.

'A vitamin pill,' she says.

'Why do I to have to take a vitamin pill if I'm eating healthy food?'

Noah looks up. He must have taken his red submarine already.

'It'll help your body adjust to all the new changes,' Mum says.

'*All* the changes? What else can't we eat?' I push the submarine around the plate.

'Chips, lollies, biscuits, white bread, sugary breakfast cereal and anything with pastry on or around it ...' she says.

I try to swallow the pill. It's impossible.

'Salt, sugar, artificial colours and preservatives ...' Mum continues.

The pill tastes like seaweed.

'Ice cream, cake, chocolate, packet soups, sauces and desserts ...'

I pick up my lunch box and leave.

Mum's just being ridiculous now.

Today is Wednesday so Alex isn't at school. He's got his first day at St Bennett's. Mrs Overbeek must have decided to come back from holidays because we have to line up for assembly as soon as the bell goes. The first class to arrive at the gym has to put the teachers' chairs out. That means *our* class because Mrs Leeman is always on time or early for everything.

When the rest of the school turns up, Mrs Overbeek announces it's a short assembly because she has so much work to do. She should have come back to school on Monday like everyone else.

'I have a wonderful announcement today!' Mrs Overbeek begins. 'Githa, our receptionist, had a lovely baby girl over the break! We're all so happy for her and her family. That means Roland will be spending the rest of the year in the office with Miss Creighton.' Everyone giggles. It's not a wonderful announcement for Roland. Someone will have to break the bad news to him when Miss Creighton is on her lunch break.

Mrs Overbeek waits for us to be quiet, then continues: 'You may have noticed, in the school grounds, that the building repairs from last semester's broken pipe are almost finished. There *are* a few things left to do, so Mr Wilson is organising a working bee for later in the term. He'll be saying more about that closer to the date.' Everyone's relieved he's not in assembly to say more about it today. Even though he's vice-principal, Mr Wilson never sits through a whole assembly anyway. He only turns up for *his* part, like a special guest.

Mrs Overbeek leans forwards and tells the Preps they're going to have an 'incursion' from Kidz Lizardz. The Preps *would* get to do the only interesting thing. Right now they're just looking confused because they don't know what 'incursion' means.

'… and lastly, sometime over the next couple of weeks, Ian will visit every class and talk about his new role at the school as Wellbeing Officer,' Mrs Overbeek announces. For some reason, that makes everyone start talking at once and she has to tap on the microphone to get everyone to be quiet.

Why doesn't she say 'be quiet' into the microphone?

Before we all escape, Mrs Overbeek reminds us about the new adventure playground. She suggests doing a quick 'self-risk-assessment' or watching another student before deciding whether we feel comfortable going on it. It all sounds a bit experimental to me. Why didn't the school buy playground equipment that's already been tested?

In class, we start our Closest Neighbours projects. I have some good ideas already. I'm going to draw a big map in the middle and stick pictures of beaches and wildlife around it because the Philippines have lots of both. If I have room, I'll include some boring things about climate and population density and stuff.

Then I see the *actual* map of the Philippines.

It is made up of seven and a half thousand islands.

Seven and a half thousand.

If I start drawing the map today, I might get it done by the time I'm fifty. Normally, I would ask Alex what to do. If he moves to St Bennett's, it'll be like this all the time. No Alex to ask. So I go and grab some of the books that Mrs Leeman has brought to class for this assignment. By the time the bell rings for lunch, I've read enough about the Philippines to write a guidebook, but I haven't written anything.

Jun, Braden and I race down to find Peta already at the wall again at recess. I'm so distracted thinking about all my worries like our spot on the wall and Alex and the Philippines, I forget about Mum's healthy eating plan until I open my lunch box. It's full of things I don't like or can't identify. There's some kind of leathery wrap made out of cabbage (yuck), miniature tomatoes (I hate tomatoes), carrot sticks, a million lettuce leaves and a meat that I think is chicken with green, oily stuff all over it.

There's also a snap lock bag full of birdseed and two dried apricots. The only edible thing in the container is a piece of banana cake but it takes almost all of recess to pick the passionfruit seeds off the top.

Before today, I took Alex *and* food for granted.

When I get home after school, there's a brand-new bike in the kitchen leaning against the empty fridge. It has a million gears and dials and looks a different colour depending on where you're standing – sometimes it's purple and sometimes it's pink. Dad appears from the hallway wearing a full-size grey lycra suit with green stripes. He looks kind of like a spotted tree frog. I can say that with authority because there's a chart showing all the endangered frogs of Victoria and New South Wales on the inside cover of my *Science Alive* workbook. The only difference is size – the spotted tree frog is six centimetres long.

Dad says the bike and suit are for cycling to work and back every day.

'How far is away *is* the warehouse, Dad?' He does the accounts there for a business that makes things out of chocolate.

'Oh, not too far … about ten, I think.'

'Ten *kilometres*?' I try not to laugh. 'You're going to do a twenty-kilometre round trip? Every day?' This is good news for my stomach. Dad gets tired hanging the washing out.

He's also bought one of those watches that records

your heart rate and blood pressure and how fast you're moving.

'It has an alarm and tells me everything I need to know,' Dad explains, clipping it onto his arm. The watch isn't telling him anything *now,* though.

So I guess he doesn't *need* to know he looks ridiculous.

The next morning, I pick a different cereal. I try to wrap the vitamin pill in a soggy flake and swallow it that way, except it starts to dissolve the minute it's in my mouth.

'Do we have to get these massive seaweed vitamins?' I ask Mum. 'You must be able to buy smaller ones.'

Mum says, 'You can. But these ones are the best. They were recommended to me.'

'Who recommended them? Poseidon?' I whisper across the table to Noah and start laughing.

'James Pond?' Noah says.

'Moby—'

'That's enough, boys,' Dad interrupts, but I notice he only has one piece of particle board this morning.

'The lady at the whole foods store recommended them,' Mum says, sitting down. 'It's the only one without sugar. Did you know that almost everything we used to eat contained sugar?'

'Well, I'm feeling better already,' Dad says. 'I can really notice a difference.'

Mum smiles at him and tips a whole pile of the grainiest-looking flakes in a bowl. She pours some watery stuff all over them and says, 'Oh! I nearly forgot!' then grabs a little sachet from the cupboard.

'Would you like some of this on your cereal, Jesse?' she asks, tearing the top off the sachet. 'It'll boost your energy and help you concentrate at school.'

I don't think it will. The smell coming from the sachet is affecting my concentration *now*.

When Braden and I get to school, Alex is waiting at the gate. I ask him what his first day at St Bennett's was like.

'It was okay,' he says. 'You don't have to put your hand up.'

'When don't you have to put your hand up?' Braden says.

'*Ever*. Like if you want to say something in class ... you just say it.'

'What happens if everyone talks at once?' I ask.

'Then the teacher has to figure out who goes first and who goes next ...'

I can't help thinking it'd be easier if everyone just put

their hand up. Especially in a school like St Bennett's where everyone knows the answer to everything.

As we walk inside the gate, Alex says, 'Oh, yeah … and we're allowed to call all the teachers by their first name. Even the principal.'

Braden and I stop walking. 'Imagine what would happen if we called Mrs Leeman by her first name?' I say.

We all start laughing. It makes me think of things so staggeringly daring and dangerous that the punishment hasn't been thought up yet.

We're still laughing when we get to the steps to our classroom building. Peta's just inside the corridor. 'What are you laughing about now?'

When we tell her, she says, 'Why is that funny? Don't you think she has a name?'

That makes us laugh even more. We *know* Mrs Leeman has a name. Peta's really smart, but she thinks funny things are just ordinary. Alex thinks ordinary things are funny. That's another reason I don't want him to go to another school. We need to stop thinking about funny things just before walking into class, though.

That is staggeringly daring and dangerous.

Inside the classroom, we all have a booklet on our desk. It's a guide for Grade 7s. All the secondary schools in our area are listed with cut-off enrolment dates and stuff. I already know what high school I'm going to – the same one as Noah. But we're allowed to miss school for the orientation tours so I'll put my name down for all of them. Mrs Leeman doesn't need to know Mum has already submitted all the forms and ordered my uniform. I turn my head upside down and see that Alex has a guide booklet on his desk even though St Bennett's have their own forms. I hope he loses them or forgets to hand them in.

Eventually we're told to put the booklets away and get on with our Closest Neighbours project.

I've figured out how I'm going to do mine. First, I'll draw a big flag in the middle. The map and writing can go around the outside. If I draw the map small enough, I won't need to draw each island individually. I'll stick lots of pictures on my project because the Philippines looks really cool and I'd like to visit one day. I'd like to visit there today, actually.

Mrs Leeman walks around to see what everyone's doing. When she gets to me, she moves on without saying anything – her highest compliment.

At lunchtime, at the retaining wall, Peta says her class are doing the same assignment except Ms Kendall has filled the board with ideas and headings and stuff.

'We have to do everything ourselves,' I complain.

'Yeah, but *your* class gets to do Jun's thing. With the flags or languages,' Peta says. 'So, it's still fair.'

'Everyone's too scared to do it though,' Braden laughs, 'because it's not Mrs Leeman's assignment.'

Peta asks Alex, 'What are you doing at *your* new school?'

'It's not my new school *yet*,' Alex says. 'I might not even go there,' he adds.

'Yeah, but you're sort of half-going now,' Braden says.

'Only to see if I like it, though.' Alex sounds angry and upset all of a sudden.

'How can you go *this* year to see how you like it? Doesn't it start in Grade 7?' Braden asks.

'It begins from Grade 5,' Alex says. 'But no one realised I was smart until we did that test last year.'

'What test?' I ask.

Jun looks up from his lunch. 'Yeah. What test?'

'You know, the one we all did with the dots. It tests numeracy and literacy and all that …'

'I know what you could've done if you didn't want

anyone to know how smart you are,' Jun says, suddenly. 'You should've got some of the answers wrong. On purpose. Then it would look like everyone else's test.'

Alex says quietly, 'I thought I did do that.'

I look over at Alex but don't say anything. Alex never blabs about other people, but I never thought about him keeping things quiet about himself.

I open my lunch box. Inside there's diced celery, tomato, carrot and shiny green things that taste like bathroom spray. The inside of the sandwich looks okay, but the bread isn't bread. It's that stiff crinkly cardboard they use to pack electronics.

CHAPTER THREE

The next day, after I leave the house, I take the vitamin pill from under my tongue and bury it next to one of Dad's flowery plants. A rose, I think. I make a long, skinny hole with a stick and put the giant pill right down the bottom. Then if it rains, it won't wash up. The plant will probably like something that tastes like seaweed. It might help it grow.

When I arrive home from school, the first thing I notice is that Milky is covered in dirt. The second thing I notice is three or four big holes in the garden where Dad's roses were. I don't know if it's okay for dogs to eat vitamin pills so I'm relieved to see the pill lying, whole, on top of a mound of dirt. In fact, there's *more* of it now. It's at least three times its original size and looks kind of soft and squishy. I don't know if that's because it's been in the ground or in the dog or both, but what matters now is that I have to get rid of it again. I wrap it in a few leaves and put it in the bottom of the compost bin in the kitchen, underneath Noah's breakfast.

It's too cold to wash the dog – all I can do is brush off most of the dirt and make him run around outside a bit. Dad won't yell at him because he always says, 'There's no such thing as a brainless dog ... only a brainless owner.' And Milky is Dad's dog.

Later that night, I get some pets of my own because Minha and her dad bring the fish and fish tank around. The tank is really cool. We put it on my desk. It takes up so much space, there isn't any room for me to do homework – which doesn't matter because I don't really do any homework.

'It's a bit bigger than I was expecting,' Mum says when she sees the tank.

'That's okay. It fits on my desk.'

'Yes, I can see that ... but where will you do your homework?' Mum says.

'It's okay,' I say again. 'I'll do it on the floor ... or on my bed.'

After Minha and her dad leave, Mum says, 'I'm glad we bought you a nice desk so that you could put fish on it, Jesse. If this affects your schoolwork, the fish go straight back to Minha's. Okay?'

'Yep.'

'That goes for looking after the fish, too. Feeding them, cleaning them … everything.'

'I know, Mum. I'll do it,' I say, sitting on my chair and staring into the tank. Mum and Dad should be pleased I'm using my desk for something. I've got a net, some cleaning stuff and a bottle of drops to put in the water to make it safe for the fish. Minha also gave me a big jar of fish food so I won't have to buy any for months. I take the lid off and give the fish some straightaway.

It's the same stuff Mum sprinkles on her cereal in the morning.

* * *

I thought Mum would forget about the healthy diet after a few days, but it's been nearly three weeks and there's still nothing edible in the house. Dad gets up early every morning, puts on his spotted tree frog suit

and rides his bike to work. He's started leaving earlier –
probably to get out of eating breakfast at home. *I* would
ride ten kilometres away from my alleged breakfast at
the moment.

At school, everyone offers me bits of their lunch, but
I feel mean taking it. Today, Alex gives me all his lunch.

'I ate during my counselling session with Ian,' he says.

'What do you mean? Your lunch is here.'

'I know,' Alex says, 'but Ian has instant noodles.'

'Really?' I start eating his sandwich. Alex's lunch
is pretty good, a cheese and salad sandwich and a
mandarin. I leave the packet of chips, though. I'd feel
guilty if I ate *all* of it.

'What flavour noodles?' Jun asks.

'Uh … chicken, beef and hot 'n spicy. I had the chicken
one.'

'Wow. Does he let you put the sachets in yourself?'
Braden asks.

'Yeah. He does the water, though, because it comes
out of the boiling water tap on the wall.'

'Isn't he a counsellor, though?' Peta asks. 'Does he
actually do any counselling?'

'Yeah,' Alex says again. 'Today he said, *if you have a
problem … sometimes the solution is closer than you think.*'

'Did he tell you where it is?' Jun says.

'No. We ran out of time. But I have to see him again next week.'

Alex watches me eat his sandwich. 'We have heaps of stuff to eat at home. I can bring some over to your house if you want?'

'Me too,' Jun says. 'I'm allowed to take anything I want out of the fridge and the cupboard.'

In the end, we decide Alex and Jun will come around after school to 'do homework'. They're *really* coming to bring me some supplies. I'd like to do something nice for them, but I can't think of anything. I might be able to think more clearly when I've eaten the supplies.

On the way home from school Mum drives past, so I get in the car to save me walking the rest of the way. She's not going home, though – she's off to the shops to buy groceries. I hope it doesn't take too long. Alex and Jun will be at my house in less than an hour's time.

Mum parks the car in the shopping centre carpark but we walk past the normal supermarket and into a shop I've never noticed before. It smells like grass clippings. Music that sounds like running water is coming out of a speaker in the corner. A lady inside greets Mum like they've been friends for a million years.

'Cait! How's the new food regime?'

'Wonderful, thank you!'

The lady has about twenty jangly bracelets on each arm. 'I bet the family have never felt better!' she says.

'Oh, yes,' Mum says. 'We're *really* feeling the benefits.'

Mum and Jangly-Bracelet Lady start talking about different kinds of beans, so I wander off to look around the shop. Everything is in jars or bags with handwritten labels. I've never heard of any of them. Chard. Quinoa. Bulgur. They sound like diseases.

The music in the shop is making me need to go to the toilet. Jangly-Bracelet Lady walks out the back and returns with an enormous sack of what looks like compost and puts it next to a few smaller bags of birdseed and grainy stuff on the counter. Now the conversation moves on to livers and bowels and what comes out of them. *Eww.*

'Of course, constipation causes all kinds of other problems ...' Jangly-Bracelet Lady says to Mum. 'Dull skin, dry hair and eventually ... you lose all your motivation!'

Mum nods. 'I totally agree. Everyone is so motivated now. Andrew's riding to work, Jesse leaves early for school and I hardly even see Noah anymore.'

I wander away before I'm asked any questions about my motivation specifically. The music in the shop switches over to bird noises. A display in the corner says the bird noises are supposed to be calming and restorative. Restorative of what, though? Maybe it's a spelling mistake and it's meant to read 'repetitive', because the same bird has chirped about a million times.

Finally, Mum says we're ready to go. Our stuff comes to $64.95!

$64.95!

I thought it would be cheaper with all the good stuff taken out of it. I wonder how many bags of birdseed a new roof costs? Now I know why we're really not going on a holiday this year. Mum makes me carry the sack of compost across the carpark. If I see anyone from school, I'll just say we're doing the working bee and are bringing our own dirt.

When we get home, Mum puts the stuff away in the cupboard. Right up the back, I can see the bottle the vitamins come out of. It's massive. There must be about eight years' supply in there. The bottle makes me think about what Ian said to Alex: '*If you have a problem ... sometimes the solution is closer than you think.*'

I have a genius idea.

I'm going to put my vitamin pills *back* in the bottle!

It's so enormous, Mum won't even notice.

Just as I'm thinking about it, Alex and Jun turn up at my house with my personal supplies. We have to sneak them past Mum as if they are explosives. Jun's brought these little dumplings his grandma makes, and Alex has a packet of chocolate creams. While I'm eating a dumpling, Alex walks over to my desk.

'Hey!' he says. 'I forgot all about the fish. What will you call them?'

'The little ones will stay One, Two and Three but I haven't decided about the boggly-eyed one …'

'What did Minha say its name is?'

'Bubbles.'

'Oh, yeah,' Alex says. 'You can't call him that. How about Google-Eyes?'

'Nah.'

'Googles?' says Jun.

'No.'

'Boggle-Eye?' says Alex.

'*No.*'

Jun says, 'I know! Einstein! Get it? *Eye*-nstein?'

'Einstein!' Alex and I say together, laughing. It's perfect.

We all peer into the tank. Einstein glides out from behind the castle to check out what's going on in my room, and then disappears again. He must like his new name. I put a little pinch of food in the corner and it literally hits One, Two and Three on the head. They look up and eat some. Einstein will eat when the other fish are finished. He likes the others, but not enough to swim around the tank with them.

The next day at school, Mrs Leeman makes us line up at the door of the gym for assembly. I know it's going to be a long assembly because there are about forty-five prams parked at the end of the seats and three rows of parents. Most of the babies and toddlers are crying, even though Mrs Overbeek hasn't started talking yet.

I wish I'd worn long pants and two shirts because we have to sit right up the back next to the open door (freezing) on the wooden floor (uncomfortable). Teachers are stationed like plain-clothes police officers all around the gym so we can't do anything interesting to pass the time, either.

Mrs Leeman says something to Alex while the rest of us sit down. As soon as she's clomped out of hearing distance, Alex leans over and tells us that he has to talk about St Bennett's in assembly. *Today*. Even worse ... he has to sit on a chair next to Mrs Leeman until he gets called up to the stage.

After Mrs Overbeek welcomes everyone, Samra (the school captain) and Jun (vice-captain) give out the awards – all five hundred of them. Just about every Prep gets one for something. Thomas Moore gets one for 'sitting quietly'. A roll of sticky tape could do that.

Then Miss Agostino takes the microphone. 'Hello, everyone! I'd just like to mention the Prep *communication folders* while we have so many parents here today. As you know, the *communication folders* are a very handy tool for *communicating* with our Prep families. But some of the folders are missing or broken. If I could take this opportunity to ask the parents to consider replacing them, that would be much appreciated.' She sits back down.

Why doesn't Miss Agostino just *tell* the parents to replace them? She should communicate that.

Next, Mrs Overbeek speaks. 'The working bee will be in two weeks' time. On Saturday morning. At 9 am. Is that right, Mr Wilson?' We all follow Mrs Overbeek's gaze towards Mr Wilson, who has just arrived by the side door. 'There's a lot to do ... trees to plant, mulch to spread, a vegetable garden to be set up for the Preps and the new breezeway toilet block has to be painted in a nice colour.'

It's a *toilet* block. Who cares what colour it is? Mrs Overbeek must have decided to talk about the working bee instead of Mr Wilson to keep the parents from getting bored and leaving the assembly.

'There will be a sign-up list placed in the foyer for any students and parents who are interested in helping,' she says.

I can guarantee there won't be anyone signing anything. None of us even want to be here during the week.

Everyone starts talking. Mrs Overbeek probably wants to say, 'be quiet' but the parents are making more noise than the kids. Eventually, Alex steps forwards and takes the microphone. The talking stops.

It looks like he's just standing there, doing nothing.

Braden leans over. 'What's he saying?'

I shake my head. 'I don't know ... I can't hear anything. I don't think the microphone is working.'

Mrs Overbeek takes the microphone from Alex and taps her finger on the top. We all nearly have a heart attack because now it's working perfectly.

Alex finishes, '… and at recess and lunch, you can join maths club or chess club. And *after* school, there's homework club and study groups.'

St Bennett's sounds like the most boring place on earth. Even more boring than here.

Mrs Overbeek says, 'Well, thank you Alex. That was very informative. You might be interested to know that I went to St Bennett's, many years ago. And it was a memorable experience.'

She doesn't mention whether it was good or not.

After another twenty years, Mr Wilson walks onto the stage after all.

'Yes, uhhh … just to finish up, I want to remind you … uhhh … that if you have any problems, anything at all, feel free to drop in on Mr Shoreham, our new Wellbeing Officer. Most of you will recognise him from the last couple of terms, but he's here to talk about anything that's troubling you. So, just remember … uhhh … his door is always open and he's always available to have a chat …' Mr Wilson trails off.

I'm expecting Mrs Overbeek to tell Mr Wilson we don't have anyone called Mr Shoreham working at the school, but maybe she wants to get the assembly over as much as we do because she doesn't say anything.

She'll have to remind him after assembly that *Ian* is our Wellbeing Officer now.

It does take a bit of getting used to.

At recess, Thomas Moore is already sitting on our wall. It's getting a bit awkward, him being around all the time, but none of us want to be mean to a Prep. Even Thomas Moore.

'Uh … Thomas?' Braden says. 'This is our spot.'

'I know,' he says.

'How are you going with the other Preps?' I ask him. 'Maybe you could eat recess with them?'

'Maybe *you* could eat recess with them,' he says.

'Isn't it more fun in the Prep playground?' Peta presses. 'With the sandpit and the digger and stuff?'

'Not really,' Thomas Moore says. 'I have to stand in line for the digger and when it's my turn, the bell goes and Miss Agostino says, "time to come inside".'

'That doesn't sound like fun,' Jun agrees.

'You *must* have a couple of friends,' Braden says.

'I have a lot of friends,' Thomas Moore says, smiling at all of us looking at him.

'How about you, Alex? Are there any nice kids at St Brainiac's? In maths club? Or chess club?' Peta teases.

Alex shifts uncomfortably on his bit of the wall. 'No, not really. There's one kid in my class I get paired up with sometimes. Kade.'

I haven't heard Alex mention him before. I wonder if Kade knows Alex's friends are *here*.

I sit down and open my lunch box. Inside there's three things: an apple, some kind of soggy slice with oats and sultanas, and a plastic container with a lid. I take the lid off and find leftovers from last night's dinner – brown rice with tuna and mixed vegetables. I pick all the sun-dried tomatoes out and eat the rice. I hate sun-dried tomatoes even more than ordinary ones. They look like ears.

At the end of the day, Mum's car is at the gate. It's actually in the bus bay even though there are proper parking spots everywhere because our class always gets out last. I stick my head through the passenger-side window where Noah is sitting and ask her to move forwards a bit.

Instead, she gets all impatient and says, 'Just hurry up and climb *in*, Jesse. I'm in the bus bay.'

When I open the door, about a million bits of paper fly out and go all over the road and everywhere. Mr Winsock, the sports teacher, is standing about five metres away so I can't just leave them. But he doesn't help me either because our car is in the bus bay.

Mum sticks her head out her window and says, '*Hurry up! I'm parked in the bus bay.*'

I'm still chasing bits of paper when the bus arrives and pulls up alongside our car. It looks miniature with a bus right next to it. The bus driver looks miniature, too, but she's got a big, angry expression on her face. She watches as I collect the remaining papers. So do all the passengers on the bus.

When I finally scramble into the car, Mum says, 'I forgot you have to see Dr Belinda today.'

How could she forget? Mum *works* with Dr Belinda. She should know when *everyone* has to see her.

When we get to the dentists' surgery we find a park right outside because Mum has a staff permit on the windscreen. I start becoming worried sitting in the waiting room. We're not supposed to be eating any sugar so Mum might get suspicious if I have any cavities in my teeth. I only just thought of that now.

While we're waiting, Noah leans towards me.

'You're going in first,' he says.

'Who says?'

'I'm just *telling* you … I'm going in after you.'

'Good,' I tell him. 'I want to be first.'

'Why?'

'Because I'd rather be sitting out here relaxing when *you* still have to go in.'

Noah says, 'Oh. Yeah. I'll be first, then.'

'Too late,' I say. 'You already said I'm first. You can't change your mind now.'

Mum leans forwards, 'Just stop it, will you? It's a *check-up*. We have six year olds that make less of a fuss than you two—'

'Cait! I didn't know you were bringing the boys in today!' Ying, one of the other nurses who works with Dr Belinda, stands in the doorway.

Mum looks up and has to pretend she's leaning forwards to grab a magazine, not because she's in the middle of telling us off.

'Oh, hi, Ying. Yep. Would you believe I nearly forgot?'

'Wow! Lucky you remembered!' Ying says to Mum, then turns to me and Noah. 'Who wants to go first?'

Noah and I both stand up. 'Whoa! One at a time!' she says, laughing. 'You can go first, Jesse.' I give Noah a big grin but it doesn't even last the length of the corridor.

By the time I'm on the recliner getting tilted upside

down, wearing a bib and sunglasses, I can't even remember why I wanted to go first.

'I'm guessing you don't have a problem with soft drink,' Dr Belinda says after a few minutes of prodding my teeth with about ten different metal things.

I know Dr Belinda's really talking about the *sugar* in soft drink because she says I have no cavities in my teeth and all I need is a 'special' clean. But why? She just said I have no cavities. I have to spend the next half an hour having my teeth sand-blasted with coarse grade spearmint gravel that goes everywhere.

After we arrive home, I do my maths homework on the floor, then sit up at my desk and watch the fish swimming around. It's getting a bit hard to see them. The water is misty and the glass has yucky green stuff on it. I google it and find out that I have to clean the tank. Already! I thought I'd only have to do it every few months or so, but it's only been two weeks. I go into the kitchen and grab a takeaway container. It's a bit sad seeing the takeaway containers in the cupboard. It reminds me of the good old days when we used to have takeaway food in them.

Back in my room, I fill the container with water from the tank. The little fish go berserk swimming around the tank and away from my net. Eventually I catch them. Einstein swims into the net straightaway, like he's stepping into a hotel elevator. In the laundry, I empty the tank, scrub the glass, wash the gravel, then fill it up with clean water from the tap and add the little drops.

It takes about twenty hours.

I leave the green slime on the treasure chest, sunken hotel and other stuff. The castle looks better a bit slimy. More authentic.

In the morning, before school, Alex and I walk down to the adventure playground instead of the wall for a change.

'How's St Bennett's?' I ask him. I'm secretly hoping that he hates it.

'It was a bit better this week,' he says. 'I know my way around and Kade said he'll help me with a maths assignment.'

It's hard to imagine anyone smart enough to help Alex with anything. Kade's brain must be the size of a watermelon.

'What does everyone *do* there, though? At recess and lunch?'

Alex says, 'Same as here. Like, yesterday, two kids climbed up on the roof and got stuck on the shade sail.

One of the teachers had to use the telescopic ladder to rescue them.'

'Did they get in trouble?' I ask.

'Not really … they had to write a paper about safety at school and present it to the class.'

I would rather have a detention than present any sort of paper to the class. But maybe our schools are more alike than I thought. Two kids got stuck up on the shade sail here, too, the other day. Mr Winsock made them throw down all the sports equipment that was up there before guiding them to safety via the downpipe. They didn't get a detention, either. They got a lamington each because there were eight frisbees up there.

Ian wanders over. 'How's it going, boys?'

'Good, sir.'

We start smiling before he even says anything. We just know it'll be funny.

'Oh, don't worry about the "sir". "Ian" is just fine.'

'Uhh … Ian, are you a teacher or a counsellor now?' Alex asks.

'Oh, well,' Ian says, 'fingers crossed that I'll be able to swap and choose. I love the teaching side but helping kids out with their troubles is really where it's at with me.'

When Ian leaves, Alex says to me, '*fingers crossed*' and starts giggling.

'I know … *swap and choose*,' I say and start laughing myself.

'*Where it's at!*' we both scream at once – it's a triple whammy.

Alex and I laugh so much we start crying.

CHAPTER FOUR

'**Y**es … hello, everyone. Uhh. Don't forget this weekend there's a working bee on Saturday,' Mr Wilson announces over the PA system. 'Uhh … that's this weekend. If you'd like to grab some tools and come to school … Uhh … there's a sausage sizzle at lunchtime.'

A sausage sizzle!

I haven't had a sausage in bread for *weeks*.

I don't want Mum or Dad to come with me, though. I'll tell them I'm going to the working bee at the last minute when they're busy doing something else. And that I'll only be there to keep Alex company.

But when I mention it to everyone at recess, Alex says he can't come.

'I'll come,' Jun says. 'If I'm allowed.'

'Me too,' Braden says. 'I'd rather do stuff here for the school than at home for no one.'

Alex looks a bit flat. 'Kade's coming to my house on Saturday to do St Bennett's homework. We have to study the Balian–Low theorem.'

I don't even know what the Balian–Low theorem is. It sounds like something Mum would make me eat instead of a sausage in bread.

After recess, Mrs Leeman hands back our Closest Neighbour projects. On the corner of mine she's written, *You really challenged yourself, Jesse. Good work!*

Does she mean good work for challenging myself, or is my *assignment* good work?

As soon as we put our assignments away, the door opens and Mr S and Ian walk in. Mrs Leeman must have been expecting them because instead of looking annoyed that her lesson has been disrupted, she nods her head at the clock, satisfied that everyone is following her schedule.

I can't believe I didn't realise last term that Ian is Mr S's son. Now that he has short hair and is wearing a proper collared shirt instead of the T-shirts he used to wear, he and Mr S look identical. I wonder if Mr S has any other sons he is trying to turn into himself.

They lean on either side of the empty desk at the front of the classroom and fold their arms in exactly the same way. It's only a single desk, so it looks a bit funny, but the only other free desk is Mrs Leeman's and she's still in the room.

Mr S starts to talk about Ian's new position as Wellbeing Officer. 'Ian will be here every day … in his own office.' He blabs on for about a week about Ian's qualifications and experience with kids. 'Ian's always had my full support and encouragement, and he's well-equipped to deal with whatever problem you might have.'

Ian says, 'I really hope you guys feel like you can swing by and have a chat anytime. My door is always open.'

It's a good thing Alex is sitting behind me because if I look at him right now I'll start laughing.

Swing by and have a chat … my door is always open.

Mrs Leeman doesn't approve of *any* kind of laughter and it would be that kind of laughing where you start and then can't stop.

After school, Braden, Jun and I go to the office to put our names on the working bee sign-up list. Miss

Creighton isn't there, so the atmosphere is quite relaxed. Roland hands us a pen to use.

'You're the first three to sign up,' he says, pleased. 'It's great to see you interested in helping out your school.' Roland is nice so we don't tell him we'll probably be the last three, and the only thing I'm interested in is the barbeque lunch.

When I arrive home from school, I can only open the door halfway. The hallway is a mess. Dad's new bike is lying on top of a mountain of brown cereal flakes, broken eggs, spilled bags of flour, and bags of assorted leaves all floating in a puddle of watery milk. Mum and Dad are arguing about something in the kitchen. It turns out he got home early and leaned his bike against the wall in the hallway, then Mum got home with the shopping and everything fell on everything else.

I head up to my room straightaway before anyone suggests I help clean up the mess. The fish tank is looking pretty murky again, so I clean that instead. After taking the fish out, changing the water and gravel, treating the water and then plonking the fish back in, I'm totally bored with the whole thing. I'll do the sunken buildings and stuff *next* time. There's a thick, green film of gunk all over them now. The castle looks like one of those abandoned castles in an old movie where plants are taking over and making it disappear.

* * *

When Braden and I arrive at the working bee on Saturday morning, it's starting to rain. Most of the parents are already there, even though it's not even 9 o'clock. Everyone is wearing a flannelette shirt and has a shovel. It looks so funny. If Mr Wilson got on the phone and ordered some concrete, we could have an in-ground swimming pool by lunchtime. Instead, he sends half the parents home to grab different tools; garden forks and paintbrushes and stuff.

Braden and I decide to paint the new toilet block. It'll be easy and it's undercover. I'm not going to work in the rain for a sausage in bread.

The cans of paint are stacked up in the breezeway. Mrs Overbeek has found a colour so boring it doesn't even have a name. 'Neutral' is too fancy a title for it. It's the same colour as the school hall, the classrooms and the breezeway. You'd want to know in advance where the toilet is because you could be standing right in front of it and still be looking around for it.

At about 9.30 am, Jun arrives with his grandparents. They've brought shovels, too, but Mr Wilson says it's too late for them to go home and get something different. Too late for what, though? Jun's going to dig the veggie patch with them. He's hoping to find some interesting old wrappers and stuff in the dirt before the boring veggies go in. Jun's collection of wrappers nearly fills up a whole wall in his room, now. He's arranged them in order of condition, with the old ones up the top leading down to the newer ones towards the floor. It looks amazing. His grandparents don't mind as long as there's no half-eaten bits of food stuck on them.

At 10 o'clock, Mr Wilson has to say, 'Uhhh, okay ... time to start,' because everyone is standing around doing nothing.

It's not so bad, painting with Braden. We slop the paint around a bit and let it drip everywhere, but it doesn't matter because we're here on a Saturday. We're already doing a punishment.

Eventually, Mr Wilson announces it's time for lunch. All the parents put their tools down and obey him like robots. Maybe they're only here for the sausage sizzle too. The Preps' veggie patch is almost finished. Jun's grandparents have done the most digging, even though they're the oldest ones here except maybe for Mr Wilson who isn't doing anything anyway.

Mr S arrives to start the barbeque. He says all the parents should have a sausage before the kids can have one. Some parents take *two* sausages. They're holding them both in one hand but I can see what they're doing. When I finally get to the table, there's only about three cold ones left, some wholemeal bread and no butter. If I want sauce, I have to go past Ian, who is guarding a pile of fried onions. When I'm closer he asks, 'How's it going, Jesse?'

What kind of question is *that* to ask someone who's at school on a Saturday?

'Okay, I guess.'

'That's the way. Doing a good job out there, I see.'

'Thanks.'

'It's a pity Alex couldn't make it today,' Ian says, 'but I think he's snowed under. St Bennett's is loading him up a bit.'

'Yeah,' I say, smiling. But somehow it's not as funny when Alex isn't here. This is the first time I've done anything like this – out of school hours – without Alex.

I look over at the tomato sauce bottle. It's almost empty. Sauce is blobbed all around the top and is running down the side. It's *gross*. Mr Wilson can't say anything about the mess because the parents made most of it. He just pretends there isn't sauce and grease and mucky used serviettes all over the trestle table.

While we're eating, Jun looks over the stuff that's been collected in the rubbish bags and dug-up mounds of dirt and clay. He scrabbles through everything and finds two really old Bezels toffee wrappers and an unopened packet of chewing gum footy cards. We can't read the writing on the footy cards but one of the older parents recognises the player on the front from the 1980s! Suddenly everyone's interested in the cards.

'Why don't we display the cards in the foyer?' Mr Wilson suggests. 'With all the trophies and awards?'

The parent who recognised the footy player says, 'What a good idea.'

'And I'll give the display an interesting title,' Jun says to Mr Wilson.

'Uhhh … I suppose so,' Mr Wilson says, already looking deflated.

'How about "Forty Years of Littering at Westmoore"?' Jun says, holding both arms out wide.

'Uhhh … no.'

'Or "The History of Littering"?'

'I don't think so,' Mr Wilson says.

'Maybe "Littering Through the Ages"?'

'All right, Junli,' Mr Wilson says. 'I don't think I have the time to be organising foyer displays. Put the cards away and uhhh … help Mr S clean up the barbeque.'

Everyone stands up and starts cleaning up the mess. It doesn't take long because after it's done, the working bee is over and we get to head home. The rain stops as soon as the clean-up is finished. Braden and I are going to walk home even though Jun says we can have a lift with him. We want to have a go on the new adventure playground while there are no kids on it.

'How many wrappers do you have? On your wall, I mean?' Braden asks, watching with interest as Jun flattens out the Bezels wrappers. He only started at Westmoore this year – I don't think he's been to Jun's house yet.

'I don't know how many. But I have from the ceiling down to about here,' Jun says, holding his hand out about knee-high.

Mr Wilson circles around the groups of parents and kids saying, 'Thank you! Thank you for coming today!' which really means, 'everyone stop talking and go home immediately'. Braden and I walk around the other side of the school towards the front gate in case Mr Wilson tells us off for not going straight home or makes us clean up something else.

There's no one on the adventure playground but there are two kids running around the asphalt courts next to the classrooms. One of them is Peta. She jogs over to where we're standing.

'Oh, good! You're finished,' she says, catching her breath.

'What are you doing?' Braden asks.

'Running.'

'Yeah, we can see that, but why?' I ask.

'We can't run around the oval today because of the working bee ...'

'Yeah, but *why* are you running?' I ask again.

'I like running,' Peta says, 'and it helps if you have someone to run with.' Peta waves her arm towards the other kid running around the asphalt for no reason. He waves back and yells out, 'Fifty-nine!'

Peta runs off towards the oval. 'I'm training with Ahmed today,' she calls back to us. 'He would come over but he's a bit shy.'

Braden and I watch her go.

Did Ahmed mean fifty-nine *laps?*

No way!

CHAPTER FIVE

'**W**hat are the Grade 7 orientation tours like?' Alex asks me one day before school.

'They're okay, I guess.'

'I wish I was going with you,' he says, looking sad. 'I don't get to do any of that stuff.'

'Well, you're not missing much,' I tell him. 'I'm probably not doing any more.'

I'm really *not* doing any more tours. All we do is walk around the school and all the kids stare at us. Also, they're kind of boring. The principal or vice-principal or whoever goes on and on about how many Bunsen burners they've got and how healthy the canteen menu is. And I already know what a uniform shop and an oval look like.

I'm happy not to be on an orientation tour today because something good is actually happening *here.* Kidz Lizardz are coming to visit the Preps – and our Grade 6 class are going to see them too. Miss Agostino can't manage the Preps and a class full of lizards on her own, so Mrs Leeman said our class would be happy to help. Even though we didn't even know about it until two minutes ago. That's why there's about twenty Preps' faces staring through the glass bit of our classroom door and no work on the board despite it being 9.03 am.

The best part is Mrs Leeman is not staying – she's going to do some work in the staffroom because she doesn't want to spend the morning in a classroom filled with snakes and lizards.

I don't suppose they want to spend the morning with her, either.

Once all the Preps are inside, Miss Agostino makes us push all the desks back so there's a big space in the middle. She tells the Preps to sit in a big circle on the floor to stop the lizards running off down the corridor. Then she tells *us* we have to make a slightly bigger circle around the Preps to stop them doing the same thing.

I hope there's a record of the desks' coordinates before we moved them. Mrs Leeman gets angry if even *one* of them is out of alignment.

It gets a bit tricky when no one will willingly sit next to Thomas Moore, who only wants to sit next to me. Miss Agostino asks the twins, Huong and Amy, to sit next to him but as they'll only sit next to each other, it would only have solved half the problem anyway.

In the end, Miss Agostino asks me and Thomas Moore to sit in the middle of the circle where the lizards and snakes are going to be. Everyone says it's not fair but it *totally* is.

It's about time I got something back for putting up with Thomas Moore since the start of the year.

The door opens and an older man wearing a park ranger-looking uniform comes in with some red plastic cages. His beard goes halfway down his chest. Following him is a lady wearing the same uniform but she's only carrying an old cloth bag. Maybe it's a bag to clean up if one of the lizards does their business on the floor.

Before the park ranger guy starts, the door opens again and Mr Wilson and Ian come into the classroom. Ian walks around to where Alex is sitting and says loudly enough for everyone to hear, 'Hey, Alex ... Your mum is coming to get some photos for the newsletter. She's just running a bit late.'

I've noticed Ian's into everyone else's business a lot more now he's the Wellbeing Officer.

The Kidz Lizardz guy introduces himself. 'Hello everyone, I'm Jacky.'

The lady steps forwards and waves. 'And my name is Bec.'

Jacky starts a long, boring lecture about reptiles. 'Today we're going to talk about where reptiles live, what they eat, how to handle them and what to do if you see one.'

We all see one, though, and want to handle it *now*.

'... and at night, the shingleback lizard finds a safe, dark place to sleep where it is protected from predators,' Jacky goes on.

Finally, he opens a red cage, takes out a shingleback lizard and hands it to Bec inside the circle. Then he takes out a frillneck lizard, a blue-tongue lizard and a Murray River turtle. He gives them to Bec, who starts to pass them around the circle. It's pretty cool because after everyone gets a turn, they come back into the middle and Thomas Moore and I get to hold them for ages while Jacky talks some more about leaves and habitats and stuff.

'All of my friends are right here in this room,' Jacky says, 'and most of them have adapted beautifully to their natural environment. They haven't needed to evolve any further for thousands of years.' He smiles at the lizards and turtles crawling all over the floor. 'Looking after them takes up all my time,' he adds.

I'm starting to see why he doesn't have any *human* friends.

After all the animals are back in the middle, Jacky lifts the red cages up over our heads into the circle and Bec places them in a row.

As she moves along the line opening all the little doors, Jacky says, 'Okay! Pay attention, everyone. I don't need to tell any of my friends where to go. What you're about to see is quite amazing!'

For a few minutes, nothing happens. Then one by one the lizards and turtles walk over to the cages. A couple of them stay there but the rest of them crawl around on the carpet until they get to Minha. They sit on the floor in front of her, on her arms and legs and on her school uniform. One of them sits on her head. Jacky's right – it *is* amazing, but Minha's been in our class since Prep. We're used to the effect she has on animals. Jacky looks more amazed than we are.

After all the lizards and turtles have been redirected from Minha into their enclosures, Jacky tests to see whether we've been listening carefully.

'Who can tell me another name for the shingleback lizard?' he asks.

'Mr Wilson!' Thomas Moore says, and everyone laughs including Mr Wilson himself because Preps are allowed to say anything.

Bec stacks the cages up at the door and we all think Kidz Lizardz is over until she steps forwards again and opens up the cloth bag. She takes out a massive, green-orange snake that's long enough to go halfway around the circle with everyone holding onto a bit.

'Blossom is a Pilbara olive python,' Bec says. 'She's over six metres long and weighs sixty-five kilos.'

I can see why they leave Blossom till last. The lizards and turtles seem a bit boring now.

After everyone has held Blossom and Bec has put her back in her bag, Alex's mum rushes through the door.

'Sorry, I'm so late!' she says to Miss Agostino. 'I got caught up in the office chatting to Miss Creighton.'

Miss Agostino must wonder what she was *really* doing. Miss Creighton doesn't chat with anyone.

Office furniture doesn't count unless maybe the printer/scanner is stuck on the 'accepts verbal commands' setting.

Alex's mum asks Jacky if he would mind taking one or two of the lizards out for a quick photo with the Preps.

'And maybe a python picture with the school captains and their Prep buddies?'

Bec agrees to let Blossom out for a few minutes to pose. Huong and Amy sit in the middle of the beanbag and Jun and Samra kneel on either side. Blossom looks happy to be out of her bag again so soon.

Everyone laughs a bit because it looks cute and funny, then everyone panics a bit because Huong starts sinking into the beanbag under sixty-five kilos of Pilbara python. Jacky puts down all his red cages so he and Bec can pick up Blossom, while Ian rushes forwards to rescue Huong. During the chaos, Thomas Moore starts jumping up and down yelling, 'Shingleback Wilson! Shingleback Wilson!'

Miss Agostino says, 'Not now, Thomas! Jacky is busy with Huong.' Even though it's actually *Ian* rummaging around in the beanbag trying to find her.

When Huong is eventually brought to the surface, Jacky gives her a Kidz Lizardz colouring-in sheet, which makes her the subject of the other Preps' envy for the second time in five minutes.

Jacky and Bec have been gone for several minutes before Mrs Leeman ventures back into the classroom. She makes Ian and Mr Wilson stay until every desk is back in its correct position. Alex's mum says, 'Well, I guess I should be going' and tries to leave but Mrs Leeman gives her a scary look so she stays and moves some desks as well.

After recess, Mrs Leeman turns something fun into something boring as usual by making us do an assignment on an endangered Australian reptile or amphibian. We have to make our own information cards – draw a picture of the endangered animal on the front and write information about it on the back.

She says, 'And I don't want to see any endangered frogs of Victoria and New South Wales.'

For a minute I think she is in favour of their extinction and *literally* doesn't want to see them, but I guess it's also possible she has read the *Science Alive* workbook. I got my copy from Noah so some of the frogs probably *are* extinct by now and belong in a book with a more appropriate title.

After a few minutes, one by one, everyone in the class notices something sitting on the windowsill. It's Shingleback Wilson. He's not in a safe, dark place as Jacky predicted, but a dangerous, light one. He must have been left behind. Mrs Leeman won't be happy to see he's still here, which is a pity because at the moment he's the most attentive member of the class. He can face the front *and* keep his eyes on her even when she walks around the room.

Mrs Leeman walks over to the pinboard and starts rearranging everything to make room for our finished cards. We're all trying to work quietly and not look at Shingleback Wilson.

After a few minutes, Shingleback Wilson leaves his position on the windowsill and starts walking up the aisle. He continues right up to the front and stops at Mrs Leeman's desk. It's evidently not this *particular* lizard that's kept his species off the endangered list. He climbs up the leg of Mrs Leeman's desk and stops nearly at the top, just with his head poking over the edge. It's amazing. His feet are really grippy.

Nobody is doing their work. We're all watching Shingleback Wilson and waiting for Mrs Leeman to turn around.

After about a hundred years, she walks over to her desk, sits down and is about to ask us why we are all facing the front and not doing our work – then she sees him.

Shingleback Wilson and Mrs Leeman are maybe twenty centimetres apart. They both have the same expression on their face. His head turns to face us, too.

Without taking her eyes off Shingleback Wilson, Mrs Leeman tells Jun to go and get Ian. I don't know why she asks for *Ian* in particular. Ian doesn't do anything without discussing it for an hour first.

After Jun leaves the room, Minha comes up to the front and sits quietly on the floor next to Mrs Leeman's desk. Shingleback Wilson steps off the desk leg and onto Minha's shoulder. He looks as though he's enjoying himself. He takes a final look around the room, walks down her arm and allows her to put him in her hoodie pocket. Everyone in the room except Mrs Leeman gives Minha a round of applause. Braden stands up and yells, 'Go, Minha!'

But Mrs Leeman has recovered now that Shingleback Wilson is out of sight. She gets a look on her face that does three things at once: 1) tells Braden to be quiet and sit down, 2) tells us to get back to work and

3) gives permission for Minha to leave the classroom immediately and return without Shingleback Wilson.

For the rest of the lesson, we keep looking around hoping to see another lizard or turtle, but Jacky must have only left one of his friends behind today.

At lunchtime, everyone crowds around Minha, asking her what happened to Shingleback Wilson after she left the classroom.

'I took him to get a drink in case he was thirsty,' Minha says. 'Then I punched some holes in the top of a plastic container so he could breathe.'

'Yeah, but where is he now?' I ask. 'Can we go and have a look at him?'

'And I put some sticks and leaves in the container so he wouldn't be scared,' Minha adds.

'But where *is* he?' Braden asks, impatiently.

'He's in the office on Miss Creighton's desk,' Minha says. 'Jacky and Bec are going to pick him up at the end of the day.'

We all wander off, disappointed we won't get to see Shingleback Wilson again.

There aren't enough sticks and leaves in the world to make it anything less than terrifying to be sitting next to Miss Creighton until the end of the day.

For a day that started so well – no Mrs Leeman, Kidz Lizardz then Shingleback Wilson staying on for a lesson with us – it's ended a bit flat. And there's nothing edible in my lunch. Today is Thursday, which means I've been given the same apple four days in a row. I know it's the same one because I marked it with a 'J'. I also have a wrap with yucky pickled vegetables in it and a snap lock bag full of driveway gravel.

CHAPTER SIX

One weekend during school holidays, I have to stay with Grandma and Grandpa. Mum and Dad are heading to Pleasant Bay to meet Aunt Melissa's baby. How can you *meet* a baby? You can't shake its hand or anything. All you can do is look at it. I think it's a long way to go to *look* at a baby. Especially this one because we've already seen about a thousand photos of it. It looks round and crinkly – the same as every other baby.

Newcastle Nanna is already there helping Melissa. I hope babies don't make any mess because Newcastle Nanna hates mess of any kind. She goes into a panic if you eat something crumbly without a plate and follows you around the house with a miniature vacuum cleaner.

Noah is staying with his friend Bree because he thinks he's too old to stay at Grandma and Grandpa's. That's fine with me. He's going home each day to feed Milky and water Dad's plants. I told him not to go near my fish. I'm giving them a weekend feeding block before I leave. Einstein will show the other fish what to do with it.

On Saturday morning, Dad drives me to Grandma and Grandpa's. Grandma's made fresh scones and there's jam and cream on the table – the proper thick cream that sits in a blob and doesn't go runny. Dad and I get a bit emotional when we see the scones. We haven't seen cream, sugar or any kind of cake for weeks and now we're looking at all three.

'Why don't you rethink this healthy living business, Andrew?' Grandma says. 'Just look at your father!'

Dad and I look at Grandpa, who is using the edge of his scone like a front-end loader, collecting the layer of cream on his plate.

'I know, Mum, but I can't be the one to back down on this,' Dad complains.

'Oh, for goodness sake!' Grandma says. 'Don't be so childish.' But I notice she gives Dad a container with about five scones in it when she thinks I'm not looking.

While Grandma's waving goodbye to Dad at the front door, Grandpa leans towards me at the table. 'After morning tea,' he whispers, 'we'll get Grandma a birthday present … at the shopping centre.'

I don't know why he's whispering because Grandma can't hear him from the front door or even from the kitchen door. She only wears her hearing aids on special occasions.

After I've eaten about a hundred scones, we head to the carport. Grandpa's car is ancient. The badges have been ripped off and the green paint is peeling off in patches all over the body. There's about a million leaves and twigs stuck in the plastic shield things on the bonnet and the driver's-side window. There's a film of dust over the whole car because it doesn't get driven much anymore. Grandpa grabs a cloth and rubs the windscreen clean. We climb in and after three or four tries, the car starts. Grandpa revs it a few times to 'warm it up'. We back out of the driveway and onto the road. Quite a few people turn to look at us. The car's engine is really loud but not in a good way and the brakes sound like fifty cats falling out of a tree. I hope the shopping centre isn't too far away.

While we're driving, Grandpa asks me how things are at school. I tell him about Alex leaving.

'Who?' he says.

'*Alex*,' I repeat, a bit louder.

'Oh, Alex! Yes ... What about him?'

'He might be going to another high school ... Without me, I mean. It's only for smart kids.'

I thought Grandpa might say, 'You *are* smart' except he's quiet for a minute.

'I see,' he finally says. 'And how do you feel about that, Jesse?'

'Well ... I don't want him to go. I wish he was staying with me.'

'Mmmm.' Grandpa turns to look at me. '*Anybody can sympathise with the sufferings of a friend, but it requires a very fine nature to sympathise with a friend's success.*'

I have no idea what he's talking about. It sounds like something Ian would say.

Grandpa continues, 'I forget who said that now – Oscar Wilde, I think. The point is ... it's harder to stick by someone doing well than someone finding it tough.'

It's not really the response I was hoping for. Also, I wish Grandpa would stop looking at me and concentrate on the road. 'Uhh, okay.'

Grandpa peers out the windscreen. 'I know you'll do the right thing, Jesse.'

That would be easier if Grandpa just told me what the right thing *is*.

We drive for a few more minutes before Grandpa swings into the shopping centre. The carpark is full of cars going around two kilometres an hour, stalking people coming out of the centre back to the place where *their* cars are parked. Grandpa slides into a space on the outer perimeter of the carpark. The spaces are nice and big, divided by yellow poles. We have to walk about fifty kilometres to get to the shops, though.

When we step off the escalator, Grandpa presses his lips together in a determined line. 'Righto, here's what we do. Look out for a shop with a lot of people inside that smells perfume-y. And make sure it's a shop that gift-wraps. If they sell cards as well, we've got the whole job covered. But let's not get ahead of ourselves. Okay?'

I nod and we head past people with prams, screaming toddlers and bunches of teenagers standing around looking at their shoes. Even though we're not making any hard turns, we're not travelling in a straight line either. Also, the floor must be sloping downwards so gently you can hardly notice it, but I know I'm *not* imagining it because people are pushing their trolleys towards us with effort – they're going *uphill*.

Suddenly Grandpa pulls me into a shop crammed full of people. The smell of perfume nearly knocks me out. Those lucky enough to be leaving the shop are all carrying a fancy paper bag with handles made of rope. I look around through stinging eyes. The whole shop is full of smelly candles and smelly candle-related things. The candles have names that don't even make sense, like 'Dawn Blossom' and 'Midnight Shine'.

A lady in a flowery apron asks us what kind of candle we want before we've had a chance to look properly at any of them. When we tell her that Grandma likes fruit, she gets too excited and uses a stepladder to bring a candle from the top shelf, even though there are literally hundreds of candles within reach. The candle she brings down isn't even a particularly fancy one. Even the name is disappointing – 'Lime 25 cm'.

'Now we need to find one for you to give her,' Grandpa says to me.

'We can't *both* give her a candle.'

'No, I suppose not. What about one of these?' He points to a wire thing with a little bowl in the middle.

'Okay, but what is it?'

'They're very popular,' the lady says. 'That is what we have in the diffuser at the moment. You put the oil in the bowl, light the candle and this lovely fragrance fills the room!'

I say 'No!' so loudly the lady jumps. I don't want to buy the smell and take it home.

The lady doesn't go away, so we need to choose something. Grandpa knows it too, although we don't say anything to each other.

'*This* looks good.' I hold up a see-through patterned globe with a candle in the middle. 'The globes have flowers or cities or triangles.'

I can tell straightaway that Grandpa likes the globe better than his candle.

'How about you give her this and I'll give her the candle?' I suggest.

'Let's forget about the candle,' Grandpa says. 'We'll get one of these nice globe things and say it's from both of us. Which one, do you reckon?'

'I like the city one,' I say, 'but I think Grandma likes patterns. How about the triangles?'

'Agreed,' Grandpa says, smiling.

Now the lady with the flowery apron will have to climb up the ladder to put Lime 25 cm back on the top shelf. She probably tries to sell it to everyone.

After Grandpa pays for the globe, we walk out of the shop with our fancy rope-handled bag. Grandpa is pretty happy. He's holding the bag so tightly I can see the white of his knuckles.

'Well?' He laughs. 'What do you think of your old grandpa now? Mission accomplished, in under twenty minutes! A record! It must be a record!' he shouts.

It's impressive but embarrassing too because people are staring at us.

When we step out of the automatic doors into the carpark though, Grandpa has another look on his face. It's the same look he gets when we ask him if he's doing online banking yet.

That's when I know we've lost the car.

I look at the rows and rows of cars in all directions. I can't see poles in any colour, let alone yellow. While Grandpa's car stands out, it's normal-sized and we're in four-wheel drive territory here – nothing smaller than a garden shed on wheels. Even if our car was two metres away, we wouldn't be able to see it unless we were on top of it.

I suggest we go back inside and ask the person at the information desk for help, but Grandpa refuses. He thinks it's less embarrassing walking around the carpark searching for the car than telling someone inside that we can't remember where we parked it. Someone who probably hears it fifty times a day. I offer to do the asking but he won't let me.

'All we have to do is start at one spot and work our way around until we find the car,' Grandpa says.

I hope he isn't planning to work his way around the whole carpark. It could take hours or even days. I guess by dinnertime Grandma will get worried and organise a search party.

Thinking about dinnertime reminds me I haven't eaten for a while. I look through my pockets. Nothing.

What we need is a drone so we can see an aerial view of the carpark. Why don't they have those at shopping centres? Maybe they do, but we wouldn't know because Grandpa would rather walk around the carpark for a week than ask for help. I should offer a service like that. Then I'll make a million dollars and never have to share a bathroom with Noah again.

By now we've trekked all the way out to the last rows of cars. It would probably be quicker to walk home and come back in Grandma's Corolla and search for the car, but Grandpa is already looking defeated. He's gone quiet and droopy-looking and the bottom of the flowery bag is all grey and dusty from where it keeps bumping on the ground.

My eyes eventually rest on something else on the ground. It's a packet of Froot Choos. *Unopened*. It's only a 'fun size' packet, which is less fun than a regular size packet, but the sight of it fills me with optimism. While I'm not going to eat them or anything – they're on the ground – I can put them in my pocket and remember the good old days, when Froot Choos and Choco-Flakes were a normal part of life and a plate of scones didn't make me feel like crying.

The little packet gives me hope. We'll find the car and get back home before Grandma calls centre management. Or the police.

I bend down to pick it up. I have to reach my hand underneath a four-wheel drive next to a—

'Grandpa! I found it!' I shout and start jumping up and down. 'The car! The car! It's over here!' Even I can't believe the Froot Choos have worked their magic so soon and so well.

Grandpa goes from flat and low to happy and excited in a few seconds. 'I told you we'd find it! We just needed a system …'

As we walk towards it though, I notice there's something different about it. It's clean. And shiny. The ancient dust and leaves are gone. Also, I realise that the yellow poles are only in one little area – around Grandpa's car and a few others. And there's a sign.

I don't know when is a good time to tell Grandpa that we're parked in a carwash and he owes them $15.50. More, if they've vacuumed it as well.

Grandpa gets into the car and it starts on the first go. It must like being clean. I jump in the passenger side and see the carwash guys behind us coughing and gasping for air in the cloud of blue grey smoke billowing out of the exhaust. As we turn out of the carpark onto the road, I know I've left it too late to tell Grandpa about the carwash. I feel really bad because it's the same as stealing, but if I say anything, Grandpa will get upset. So we drive out of the shopping centre carpark as fugitives on the run.

Now I hope the shopping centre *doesn't* have an aerial view of the carpark.

That night I can't sleep because I'm so worried about the $15.50. I creep into the kitchen for a drink and find Grandma sitting at the table doing a crossword.

'Jesse! What's the matter? Are you feeling okay? Is your bed warm enough?'

I wish she wouldn't ask me those things. I'm scared she'll be angry with me when I tell her why I can't sleep, so I wait until she walks over to the fridge. But she's not angry at all.

'I'm *so* proud of you,' she says, coming over to give me a big hug and a kiss on the top of my head. 'And I can assure you, there's plenty of people who've taken fifteen *million* dollars from others today and are sleeping like babies.'

'Really? Who?' I ask, interested.

Grandma puts a cup of chocolate milk in front of me. 'Let's just say, I don't think you're cut out for a career in politics.' She smiles.

I feel my eyes grow heavy.

'Can I save this for breakfast?' I ask, looking at the chocolate milk.

'Off to bed now, Jesse. I'll sort out the carwash money in the morning,' Grandma says, sitting down at the table.

'Our little secret,' she adds, going back to her crossword.

CHAPTER SEVEN

Mrs Overbeek must be in a hurry today because she starts morning assembly without even waiting for everyone to be quiet. 'Term 4 is so busy!' she begins. 'I don't know how we're going to fit everything in!'

Some of the Preps are still standing up. They file into the gym okay, but don't know what to do when they get here. Miss Agostino has to shuffle down the row about three times before they're all sitting down.

'I'd like you all to welcome Ms Janik,' Mrs Overbeek says. 'She is our new student teacher and will be working in Mrs Leeman's class this term.'

Everyone turns to stare at the lady sitting on a chair in front of the fire exit. Maybe no one has asked her to move because it's her first day. I think Ian should offer Ms Janik the chair next to his. He can't have already forgotten what it's like to be a student teacher and not know where to sit or what to do.

'Also, a very big thank you to Mr S,' Mrs Overbeek says, 'who will be staying on a bit longer at Westmoore. We're so fortunate that he is able to do that for us.' Mr S stands up from where he's sitting with the other teachers and gives a little wave. Mrs Overbeek should ask him to return the retirement gift we gave him last year until he actually leaves.

Mr Wilson steps forwards and takes the microphone from Mrs Overbeek, who disappears behind the curtain.

'Uhh, hello everyone. Thank you, Mrs Overbeek.' Everyone laughs because Mrs Overbeek has already left the gym. We can see her out the side door marching across the courtyard towards the office.

Mr Wilson takes some scrunched-up pieces of paper out of his suit pocket then goes on for about fifty hours about all the things we have to do this term.

'And uhhh, just to finish up …' Mr Wilson says, 'I'd like to mention our wonderful Grade 6s. They will be having their graduation assembly at the end of the year. Very exciting. Now, I'll hand over to Mr Winsock …

I believe he wants to have a word about, uhhh … cross-country training.'

So, we're not finishing up at all. We still have to listen to Mr Winsock trying to get us interested in another kind of sport.

Everyone fidgets on the floor as Mr Winsock messes around with the microphone stand. While he's doing it, Peta stands up and walks towards the front.

Peta!

What is she doing?

Peta takes the microphone out of the stand. As she starts to speak, I discover she's been running around for fun before school as well as at the weekends!

'We meet at eight o'clock in the morning and do four laps around the oval,' she says to everyone. 'So if you want to join us this Friday for practice, it's really good fun. After we run, we have enough time to get changed and have some breakfast before school starts.' She jumps off the stage instead of going down the steps and joins the rest of Ms Kendall's Grade 6 class.

Peta's going to be disappointed. Why would anyone want to get up early and run around the oval if—

Wait.

Breakfast?

When we arrive back at the classroom after assembly, Ms Janik is already sitting in front of the supply cupboard in our classroom. She's smiling, so she must have only met Mrs Leeman today. I wonder if teachers have to write reports about student teachers? If they do, I hope Ms Janik doesn't really want to be a teacher or has a plan B of some kind.

At recess, I look for Peta to ask her about cross-country.

She seems really happy I'm asking her about training. 'You should do it, Jesse. It's really good—'

'Do you get toast or cereal?' I ask.

'What? Oh. Toast. So I'm trying to get Ahmed to join us. He's a really good runner but he—'

'Is it *white* bread though? Or multigrain? And what do you get to put on it?'

'Umm. Both. And jam or Vegemite, I think. Anyway, it takes ages to run around the oval four times. At first. But after a while, you get better. I can do it quickly now.'

'Does the jam have bits in it?' I ask.

'It's not running *fast* – just like jogging speed. Then at breakfast we can have orange juice or a hot chocolate.'

Hot *chocolate?* We didn't even get hot chocolate at home *before* the birdseed diet.

I'm going to start on Friday.

After recess, Mrs Leeman sends Jun and me to the office to hand in a big envelope. It's sealed so we can't see what's inside, even when we hold it up to the window. It's pretty thick so it's probably all the detention slips Mrs Leeman has issued, even though the term only just started. Miss Creighton is already arguing with someone else in the office, so we have to wait our turn.

'I don't understand it,' a lady is saying. 'I filled in the forms and gave them to her class teacher. I don't know what happened to them.'

'Well, you'll just have to do it all again,' Miss Creighton says. 'Roland, organise some replacement forms!' she yells. And then, to the lady, 'I can't do anything here until we have those forms.'

There's a girl standing next to the lady. She's about our age, wearing an ordinary T-shirt and jeans.

'I'm so sorry,' the lady says to Roland as he comes out from the back of the office. 'We've only just moved. Everything's still in boxes. It's so much better with Rey at the new Children's Centre at the hospital, but it's absolute chaos at home. I couldn't find the toaster this morning!'

'I didn't realise the Children's Centre was open yet,' Roland says, surprised.

'Well, not *officially*,' the lady explains, 'but they're already taking patients. And next week my mother and sister are coming over from the Philippines to give us a little more support. It's going to be so—'

'Roland!' Miss Creighton yells out from her desk. 'You're not here to stand around talking. Have you found those forms yet?'

Roland opens a cupboard and hands the lady a form from a stack of about five thousand and gives her his own personal pen to use. 'Please don't worry about Rey's enrolment forms,' he says. 'We'll sort it out.'

Jun and I glance at each other. It hasn't taken Roland long to perfect his calming voice, but I guess it's kind of essential if your job is being nice *for* horrible people (Miss Creighton) and trying to be nice *to* horrible people (Miss Creighton).

Roland glances over and sees me and Jun holding the big envelope. 'Hold on! Hold on! Here they are!' he shouts, holding his palms in the air. 'Thank you, boys.' He takes the big envelope from us.

Miss Creighton looks up from her computer and directs some non-verbal communication at Roland.

He should really know by now that the only raised voice permitted in the office area is her own.

* * *

For the next few days, Ms Janik stays in front of the supply cupboard and watches Mrs Leeman teach the class. By now, Ms Janik must be wondering why she chose teaching as a career. Maybe we should tell her about the door at the back of the supply cupboard that opens out into the courtyard.

On Thursday morning, she has the class by herself for the first time. She looks a bit nervous. We're *all* a bit nervous because Mrs Leeman sits up the back the whole time.

Ms Janik says, 'Now! Listen up, everyone! I've got a *very* exciting project we're going to work on for the rest of the term! Great Australians …' she leaves such a long pause I think she means *we* are Great Australians, but she means we have to do a *project* on a Great Australian.

'I'm putting you into groups of four … and one group of five … and each group will research a Great Australian. Tomorrow, Friday, we will start making a visual presentation to support your class presentation at the end of term. So if the group leaders would like to come up and choose an envelope with a name inside …'

Nobody moves because we don't know what group we're in or who the group leaders are. Mrs Leeman must give Ms Janik one of her instructional gestures because Ms Janik continues. 'Oh! Sorry! So … if you'd like to get into groups of four and one group of five and elect a leader to collect an envelope …'

Half the class slowly stands up. We can't believe our luck. Mrs Leeman would never in a million years let us do a group project with our friends, but Ms Janik seems to have forgotten the only thing she had to do other than tell us she's going to put us in groups was to *put* us in groups. Everyone kind of shuffles towards their friends and stands in little clusters. Group leaders are not so much elected as handed the position in the form of an envelope.

I'm handed the envelope for our group. It says 'Professor Fred Hollows'. Even Alex has never heard of him. I hope he was an explorer. More specifically, I hope he discovered New Zealand because we've had a map of New Zealand on the wall in the kitchen for as long as I can remember. It's got all the details about climate, population, politics, and stuff around the outside.

A few minutes before the bell goes for recess, Mrs Overbeek comes in with Rey – the girl Jun and I saw in the office the other day. She's wearing a school uniform now.

Mrs Leeman introduces her to the class and gives her the spare seat up the front. That seat isn't *really* a spare. If Mrs Leeman thinks someone is misbehaving in class, they have to sit in that seat for the rest of the lesson, so it's almost always occupied. Mrs Leeman chooses Minha to help Rey settle in but not right *now* because Minha's Great Australians group already has five members. So Rey is put in our group.

I notice Mrs Leeman's decisions overrule any of Ms Janik's arrangements.

Thomas Moore and Huong are already sitting on the retaining wall by the time we get there at recess.

'Miss Agostino might be wondering where you are,' I say hopefully.

'She knows I'm here,' Thomas Moore says. 'She said as long as I stay with you, it's okay.'

Miss Agostino didn't ask if it's okay with *me*. She should check before handing over her responsibilities. The only reason I don't tell Thomas Moore to leave is I don't know how to do it in a way that's not mean, and that will make him go away and not come back.

Mrs Leeman stares at all of us with more intensity than usual when we come in after recess. Eventually she says, 'Minha. I want you down the front next to Rey ... you'll have to swap desks with Braden for now.'

Braden's head turns around like it's spring-loaded. Minha's desk is right up the back, in a low-visibility position. He lifts his desk lid up and piles his arms up with the mess of papers, pencils and other items he has in there. Erasers, toffee wrappers and pencil shavings scatter all over the floor. Mrs Leeman allows Jun and me to help him pick everything up because Minha is already packed up and patiently waiting for his desk to be vacated.

'I may have to move you again, Braden,' Mrs Leeman says, 'so don't get too comfortable.' I turn my upside-down head a little bit to look at Braden in his new position.

He looks comfortable already.

* * *

My alarm goes off in the middle of the night on Friday. I look at my clock and remember I'm having breakfast at school and doing my first cross-country training session today. I'm up early enough to see Dad about to leave the house on his bike. It's interesting that he chose a spotted tree frog suit when he works at a warehouse full of chocolate tree frogs and other chocolate stuff. Maybe it's a silent protest against our new restrictive diet.

I have to walk to school, so I've already used up a whole lot of energy before I start. I'm surprised to see nine other kids already there – one of them is Ahmed. He's trying without success to stand next to Peta, who is jumping around all over the place. Mr Winsock makes us use even *more* energy by doing stretches.

'Okay,' Mr Winsock finally says, 'I want everyone doing four laps of the oval, except Jesse and Ahmed. I don't expect any newcomers to keep up with the others just yet. You two can just do three laps today.' Peta and Ahmed start giggling when Mr Winsock says that.

He blows his whistle and we all take off. I jog for about half a lap before the others (including Ahmed) pull away from me. I walk the second lap and spend the third lap half-walking, half-standing bent over with my hands on my knees, concentrating on staying alive. When I get to the finish line, I lie down in the damp grass, admire the swirly clouds and listen to the yells and laughing of the rest of the school arriving now that it is a civilised time of day.

A little voice that might be mine whispers, 'I think I can do another one' but Mr Winsock says, 'Not today, Jesse. I'll let Mrs Leeman and Ms Kendall know you two will be a little late to class.' I sit up and see Peta waiting for me.

It's not until later when I'm sitting in class that I remember about breakfast. Running around the oval this morning forced thoughts of toast and hot chocolate to go from the front of my mind to right out of it.

On Saturday, Alex comes over with some more chocolate creams *and* a vanilla slice. I eat the vanilla slice straightaway but put the unopened packet of chocolate creams in a gumboot under my bed.

'Fred Hollows was an eye doctor,' Alex says, peering into the fish tank. 'I went to Kade's house after school and his dad had a whole book about him. Look at all these awards he won.' Alex holds the page open. 'It says here that he stopped hundreds of people from going blind in Australia and then went all over the world doing the same thing for thousands *more* people. Pretty cool.'

'I didn't realise you and Kade were friends,' I say, feeling weirdly uncomfortable.

'We're not, not really,' Alex says awkwardly. 'We're just in the same class.'

Einstein swims forwards to look at the book. We sprinkle a bit of food in the tank and he waits in front of the castle while One, Two and Three eat the flakes as they fall through the water. They still haven't figured out that if they stay in one spot, they can keep eating. They must swim around and think, *Yay! Some food just fell on my head.*

We find out some more stuff about Fred Hollows before he became an eye surgeon. He was actually born in New Zealand, so I might be able to use the map on our kitchen wall after all.

'Hey!' Alex suddenly says. 'I've just thought of something. *First*, your brother had an eye operation, *then* you got Einstein with the boggly eyes from Minha and *now* we're doing a project on a Great Australian eye surgeon! *That's three eye things!*'

'Oh, *yeah*. What does that mean?'

'I don't think it means anything,' Alex says. 'It's just a coincidence.'

'Aye,' I say, laughing.

'Aye, aye,' Alex says.

'Aye, aye, aye,' we both say, cracking up.

CHAPTER EIGHT

On Monday morning, Mr S comes down to the oval before school to watch the cross-country training.

'This looks like terrific fun!' he says, before we've even started running. Mr Winsock blows his whistle and I jog around the oval until my legs turn to jelly.

Afterwards, in the canteen, Peta makes me a hot chocolate, but I can only take little sips like someone rescued after two weeks lost in the outback. I can't face a piece of toast.

Later, in the classroom, everyone starts working in their Great Australians groups. Everyone except *our* group. Jun, Braden and I start talking about drawing eyes with yucky diseases on our poster.

Rey says, 'It's not a project about eye diseases. It's about Fred Hollows.' She's not shy like some new kids.

'Yeah,' Alex agrees. 'It's a Great Australians project.'

I say, 'But that's what Fred Hollows did to become a Great Australian. Treated eyes that had eye diseases.'

'They're not all *diseases*, though,' Rey says. 'Some of them are eye *conditions*. That's different.'

'What do you mean?' I ask.

'I know!' says Braden unexpectedly. 'Like cataracts!'

I start laughing. 'You mean like Cataract, your *cat*?'

'*Yeah*. I mean – no.' Braden laughs too. 'Cataract is just her name. But *cataracts* are something wrong with your eyes. I don't know what they are, though.'

'It's when the eye goes kind of cloudy,' Alex explains. 'You have an operation to have the cloudy bit taken out and a clear bit put in. Fred Hollows is famous for doing that operation … he did millions of them.'

Ms Janik comes over to see how we're going. We're not going well. 'I'd like to see something on the page by the end of this session, please,' she says.

As soon as she walks away, Jun has a good idea. 'You know how tracing paper is kind of see-through?'

'Yeah,' Alex says, slowly.

'How about we draw a big eye in the middle of our poster, then have an eye-shaped flap of tracing paper over the top? *Like a cataract!*'

We all try to picture what he's describing.

'Anyone looking at our poster can lift up the *cloudy* eye and see a *healthy* eye underneath!' Jun adds.

We all agree it's worth a try and better than what we have now – which is nothing.

At the end of the morning session, Ms Janik is pleased we're starting on our project. 'It's terrific!' she says, lifting the tracing paper 'cataract' to reveal the coloured eye. 'It has real flair!'

We haven't started writing anything yet, though. It's all flair and nothing else.

At recess, Thomas Moore is at the wall, this time with Huong *and* Amy. I'm glad they seem to be friends again, but I hope that all the Preps don't come down here. Thomas Moore keeps glancing towards the end of the wall.

'What are you doing?' I ask him.

'You just missed him.'

'Who?'

'He lives in there,' Thomas Moore says, pointing to a hole at the end of the wall. 'Shingleback Wilson.'

We all take turns peering into the hole. I can't see anything – just an empty space. Thomas Moore puts half a ham sandwich on a bit of flat rock in front of the wall. I'm tempted to grab it myself.

Peta tells us that her Grade 6 class is doing the Great Australians project as well.

'I didn't know your class had a student teacher,' Braden says.

'We don't,' Peta says. 'We're doing the project with Ms Kendall.'

'Oh. We thought it was Ms Janik's idea,' Jun says.

Peta laughs. 'No. It's kind of fun, though. We get to push all the desks back and work in the middle.'

'We have to work up the front,' Braden says. 'Or in the aisle.'

'Ms Kendall doesn't mind if we talk,' Peta continues, 'as long as we're working on our projects, too.'

I think about how much fun it must be in Ms Kendall's class. We're allowed to talk in our groups, too, but only if it's *about* our projects.

Huong and Amy wander off, but Thomas Moore doesn't go with them.

'What are you all talking about?' he asks me.

'Our Great Australians projects.'

'Oh,' he says. 'My nanna's a Great Australian.'

'Why? What did she do?'

'She gave all her things away.'

'Gave what away?' Jun says.

'*My* house and *your* house and this school and the hospital …' Thomas Moore spreads his arms right out. 'And the shops and all the books in the library and the *actual* library,' he goes on.

'Why have we never heard of her?' Alex asks.

'*I've* heard of her.'

'That doesn't make her a Great Australian.'

'What *does* make you a Great Australian?'

'You know,' Braden explains. 'When you've done something amazing … and everyone knows who you are.'

'Everyone knows who I am,' Thomas Moore says.

'*That's* true,' Peta says. 'I might actually miss you next year, Thomas.'

'Where are you going?'

'Not just me. *All* of us. To high school,' Peta explains.

Everyone's quiet for a minute, then Braden says, 'It's weird to think we're all going to high school next year.'

'Yeah,' I say. 'I have to travel by bus.'

'Which one?' Braden asks.

'The forty-two.'

'Me too! But aren't you going to Claremont Park? Where are you getting on?'

'At the corner then change at the station,' I tell him. 'Two buses.'

'Me too! Change at the station, I mean. If I go to Kallista. If I go to Claremont Park, we can go the whole way together.'

'I'm going to Claremont Park too, but I'll be getting there early,' Peta says. 'They have athletics before school.'

'Maybe we could all meet at the station after school?' Braden suggests.

'Maybe.' Peta sounds unsure.

The only one not talking about high school is Alex. If he goes to St Bennett's he'll travel by train or car. St Bennett's is about a thousand kilometres away. In the other direction.

Lunchtime is nearly finished by the time Jun arrives and sits down on the asphalt.

'Samra and I had a school captains meeting with Mrs Overbeek,' he says, opening his lunch box. 'We have to do a speech at graduation assembly and thank all the teachers.'

We wait for him to go on.

'I told Mrs Overbeek that I don't want to give teachers flowers. Flowers just die,' he continues. 'So I put forward a motion for pot plants.'

'And?' Peta asks.

'Mrs Overbeek told me the flowers have already been ordered,' Jun says, taking an apple out of his lunch box.

Alex nods his head, slowly. 'So, you have to give the teachers flowers?'

'Not necessarily,' Jun says. 'I told Mrs Overbeek that the flowers she ordered won't have been cut yet. So we still have time.'

Peta starts laughing. 'What did Mrs Overbeek say when you told her that?'

'She said she didn't want to discuss it any further,' Jun admits.

On the way back to class, I see Minha and Rey in the Preps' veggie garden. It looks like they're talking to a bunch of leaves. I catch a bit of their conversation.

'Yeah, so snails and slugs are both gastropods, which means, "stomach foot",' Minha is saying, 'and they eat with thousands of microscopic teeth.'

Eww, gross.

Rey looks kind of interested in snails' teeth, though. She picks up a snail and stares at it. Minha might have to explain what 'microscopic' means. By the end of the week, Rey will know everything about snails and birds and insects but have no idea where the library is.

At the end of school, Alex, Braden and I leave via the retaining wall because Braden forgot his jumper down there.

When we're about ten metres away, Alex stops abruptly. 'Hey! *Look!*' He points to the flat rock.

A shorter, fatter Shingleback Wilson is sitting about three-quarters out of the hole in the wall, picking at Thomas Moore's sandwich.

We creep slowly towards the wall, but he scoots back into his hole as soon as one of us steps on a crunchy leaf.

'What do you think he's doing?' Braden asks.

'What do you mean?' Alex laughs. 'He's not doing anything. He's just living. He lives in the wall.'

'And we live *on* the wall,' Braden says, laughing too. He grabs his jumper and we head home.

Braden and I leave Alex at the corner and turn down our street. A really long truck is backing out of my driveway. A big sticker on the side says, 'R & J Saunders. Roof Supplies. *We're on top of it.*'

Hilarious.

Up on the roof, three people are wearing harnesses with complicated-looking toolbelts. One of them is yelling instructions at the other two.

Braden says, 'Hey, Jesse! Check this out!' and points to a massive pile of corrugated iron and roof insulation in our garden. The corrugated iron is all twisted and rusty with big holes in it. No wonder the roof leaked. Next to it the old insulation is all bunched up and it stinks. Every kind of creature has probably been up there scratching and peeing and pooing for about fifty years.

R & J Saunders have left the new stuff over by the fence. It's just a tiny pile of metal sheeting and one roll of insulation. One roll! They'll have to go back to get the rest. They weren't *on top of it* this time.

When we walk into the house, we find Mum sitting at the kitchen table with Braden's mum, Rina. It sounds like the roofers are going to crash through the ceiling at any minute.

'Rina's offered to have you at their place for the night, Jesse. You may as well keep your uniform on – just grab your pyjamas and toothbrush and stuff.'

I groan. 'Why can't I stay here?'

'It won't be finished today. They're squeezing us in between jobs.'

'I don't mind—'

'Just get your things, will you? I don't have time to argue.'

That's not really true. It would only take about ten minutes to argue. Probably less because Braden and his mum are here.

Braden follows me to my room. It's so bright in here we have to squint our eyes.

'Oh, wow. It's so *weird* in here without the roof,' Braden says, looking up. 'It feels like a giant is going to reach in and grab us.'

The light is flooding every corner of my room. I can see the space between my desk and the wall and it's like a time capsule of my life. There's stuff back there I haven't seen since kindergarten: a certificate from when I was in the Under 6s, a plastic giraffe from the spring festival and a pair of socks with different-coloured toes I've been looking for since Grade 1 … all with about a metre of dust on them.

I throw some stuff in my schoolbag, and then look for my sleeping bag in the linen cupboard. I can't find the good one. All I can see is an old one, right up the back with all the stuff we don't use. What I *do* find, when I pull the sleeping bag out, is a big box of chocolate frogs from Dad's work. *A whole box!* So Dad is telling us how great this diet is and he's cheating! The box is empty though so he must have eaten them all. I push the box back where I found it. I don't want *Dad* to know that *I* know.

Mum wants us to go to Braden's straightaway. She won't even let us stay and watch the roofers.

'I'm sorry, boys. Not this time.'

How many *other* times will we get the roof done?

Before we leave, I run back up to my room and put an old towel over the fish tank in case something falls in it. Also, goldfish eyes might be really sensitive to light and I don't know if Einstein can squint his boggly eyes or not.

Mum makes us take some carrot cake with us. 'Carrot is very good for your eyes,' she says to Rina.

'Is that right?' Rina says, impressed, accepting half the cake. She's welcome to have my share. I'll be able to see through walls if I eat any more.

Braden's house is only a few houses up from ours so it doesn't take long to get there. The lounge room and hallway are covered with a million toys and books because Braden has three little sisters. They're watching something noisy on TV and making Cataract the cat run around after a milk bottle top. When she stops moving, I get a quick look at her eyes. I remember now – they're kind of wonky but not cloudy, like *real* cataracts.

Braden and I go up to his room. He has some pretty cool stuff. He keeps most of his games in a box with a combination lock so his sisters don't get to them and spill food on them. We've only been playing for about a minute when his mum yells that dinner is in five minutes.

Five minutes!

I look at my watch. It's only six o'clock. That's about the time someone in our house says, 'Well, I guess we'd better start thinking about dinner.' *Start* thinking.

We head down the hallway to wash our hands, but Braden's sisters are already in the bathroom, taking forever. I wonder what we're having for dinner. It can't be any worse than what I get at home.

Braden's dad, Brian, is in the kitchen. He looks like Braden, only gigantic. He makes everything in the kitchen look too small. His hair is the same orange as all the kids and he has a massive beard that goes out to the sides as well as down. He takes my hand and shakes my whole arm up and down. 'Jesse! How are you today?'

'Fine thank you, Brian! How are *you* today?'

'Fine! Fine! Priceless!' Brian shouts, gripping my

hand even harder. I hope I never say anything funny when he's shaking my hand.

Rina says from the cupboard where she's counting plates, 'I hope you like lamb shanks, Jesse.'

I hope I like lamb shanks too. I don't even know if I like any kind of shank.

Everyone sits down at the table. I sit in the only vacant chair and a plate is put in front of me. There's peas and potato and I think pumpkin, which is okay, but I'm no closer to knowing what a lamb shank is, even now when there's one right in front of me. It *looks* like a mountain troll's elbow.

Lucky for me, everyone else likes shanks because after I've pushed it around the plate a few times, Brian adds it to his gargantuan meal. Rina fills the space on my plate with more potato. It's mashed with real butter and salt. And there's tomato sauce on the table. It's the first proper dinner I've had for ages.

After dinner, everyone watches the TV. For some reason, no one turns on the light so it's too dark to do anything else anyway. After a while, Rina takes Braden's sisters to have a bath and get ready for bed. Sometime later she pokes her head back in the door and asks me if I want a blanket.

'No, thank you. I'll be okay.'

'Are you sure, Jesse? It's no trouble.'

'I'm fine.'

After that, she disappears and doesn't come back. Braden and I head to his room and muck around until Brian comes down the hall and says, 'Boys? Bed!' Braden packs up his stuff straightaway! Noah and I pack up on maybe the third request.

As I climb up to the top bunk Braden says, 'Okay if I turn the light off?'

'Yep.'

'Because otherwise I have to get back up and do it.'

'It's fine,' I say.

'We don't have to go straight to sleep. We're allowed to talk,' Braden adds, climbing back into the bottom bunk. Neither of us says anything for a while.

Suddenly, Braden asks, 'Do you think Alex will go to that brainy high school?'

'I hope not,' I say, surprised to hear my own voice say it out loud.

'Why?'

'I thought we'd be at the same school next year,' I tell him.

Braden pauses for a bit. 'But what if he wants to go there?'

'I suppose that's different.' I hadn't even thought about Alex wanting to go to St Bennett's before. 'We've been friends since Prep,' I say. 'We've always done stuff together.'

'Oh. Well, I've been to lots of schools,' Braden says.

'Really?'

'Yeah,' Braden says. 'It's hard at first, when you start at a new school. It's good if you keep doing stuff with your old friends.'

I think about that; about being Alex's *old* friend.

It takes me ages to fall asleep. It's too dark and quiet. All the shapes in Braden's room are different. I don't get how a place can be so strange when it's only four houses away from home.

In the morning, as I'm getting ready for school, I think Brian is impressed I'm leaving early because I have cross-country training.

'Cross-country! That sounds like fun, Bray. What do you reckon?' he says. I don't tell him the *real* reason I do it. Or that I can barely stagger around the oval three times before collapsing on the grass.

Braden says, 'Uhh, yeah, Dad … maybe.'

But I know he doesn't mean it. Why would he? There's normal toast *and* raisin toast as well as cereal and milk on the table for breakfast.

CHAPTER NINE

It's been two weeks since we were given our assignment and our Great Australians poster still doesn't have any writing on it.

Next session, we all stare at the pile of books and page of resource links Ms Janik has given us.

I feel that, as group leader, I need to suggest something. 'How about we choose one topic each, then write about that thing on the poster?'

'It'd be funny if we all thought of the same topic,' Braden says.

I hadn't thought of that.

Rey says, '*I* know. We think of topics together and write them down on a piece of paper. Then we cut up the paper and pick one without looking.'

'*Yes.*' I smile at Rey gratefully.

Alex says, 'Okay, let's get started then. In the front of Kade's book, there's a—'

'Kade's book isn't the only book,' I interrupt. 'There's a million books.'

'Yeah, but have you read any of them?'

Everyone goes quiet. Alex and I say these kinds of things all the time as a joke but *this* time it doesn't feel jokey at all. Eventually, Rey, Jun and Braden start writing down topics on a piece of paper and then cut it into squares. I get 'Fred Hollows' early life' – before he became a doctor. I wonder if Fred Hollows was ever group leader of a project in Grade 6 and fought with his best friend over nothing? Probably not. Fred Hollows would have been the Alex of the group – already amazing, heading for the St Bennett's of eyes.

While we're working, Alex and Jun are called up to the office. Everyone looks a bit surprised because Alex never breaks any rules. I'll have to ask him what's going on at lunch.

When Peta, Braden and I get down to the wall, Jun and Alex are already there with their lunch.

'I had another school captains meeting,' Jun says. 'This time it was with Mr Winsock about Athletics Day.'

I start picking the passionfruit seeds off my banana cake. I hate passionfruit seeds. They look like tadpoles' eyes.

'Samra and I have to present the House Cup at Athletics Day,' Jun continues, taking the lid off his lunch box.

'And?' Peta asks.

'I said, "No, thank you".'

Peta laughs. 'What did Mr Winsock say to that?'

'Oh, not much. He said Samra can present the House Cup on her own.'

We all look at Jun calmly unwrapping his lunch.

'I told Mr Winsock it's not fair that one House wins just because some kids run faster or whatever,' he says. 'Those things are not important.'

A few minutes later, Thomas Moore and Huong turn up. They arrange some pieces of apple and half a ham sandwich on the rock.

'Do lizards eat ham sandwiches?' I ask him.

'This one does,' Thomas Moore says, 'but he also likes snails and spiders and insects.'

'How do you know all that?'

'Jacky told us, remember? You weren't listening carefully.' He peers into the hole in the wall.

'Ha-ha, he's got you there,' Braden says, laughing.

'What are you going to call him, Thomas?' Peta asks. 'You found him. So you get to name him.'

'Shingleback Wilson,' Thomas Moore says straight-away.

'How about Wilson *Two*?' Peta suggests. 'Then we won't get confused.'

'I suppose so,' Thomas Moore says, scrunching up his eyebrows.

We all peer inside the hole. Wilson Two is hiding right up the back. I wonder if he knows we're talking about him.

'Why don't you take your lunch over to where the other Preps are?' I say to Thomas Moore and Huong when Wilson Two doesn't come out.

'Because we like it here with you,' Thomas Moore says, peering further into the hole.

'Yeah, but we won't be here next year,' I remind him. 'We're all going to be at high school.'

'Huong will be here,' Thomas Moore says, looking up at me. 'What about Huong?'

I look over at Huong, edging her way off the wall, about to run.

'I know, but it's good to have more than one friend …'

'I do have more than one friend,' Thomas Moore

says, standing up. 'I have—' he counts along the wall, '—six friends!'

'Wow,' Peta says, impressed. 'You're pretty smart for a Prep.'

Thomas Moore grins at me. I know he's smart, but is he smart enough to know how soon the rest of us will be leaving? We're already more than halfway through Term 4.

After we've finished our lunch, I hang back with Alex while the others walk ahead. I want to ask why he was called up to the office.

'It was nothing,' Alex says. 'I had to see Ian.'

'Oh, okay. What for?'

'He wanted to talk to me about some stuff …'

'What kind of stuff?'

Alex is quiet, then gives me a sidelong glance. 'Uhh … he said if I didn't feel like noodles, I could have something from the canteen.'

'*That's* what he wanted to talk to you about?'

We stop walking.

'He asked me if I'm enjoying the difficult work at St Bennett's,' Alex says, looking uncomfortable, 'and what it's like to be around other kids … you know … like me.'

'Oh.'

We start walking again.

When I get home later that day, I finally do a bit of my own research about Fred Hollows. But I keep getting distracted by the fish – wondering what they're thinking, swimming around the sunken treasure and all the other stuff. The castle is totally green now. It could be anything – ancient ruins, a haunted house, a castle, a boarding school. It could be St Bennett's. I wish it *was* St Bennett's. Then Alex wouldn't be able to find it and he'd have to stay at Westmoore. We could do the same thing and have the same friends. Everyone would do the same work. St Bennett's has wrecked everything.

I move my homework stuff onto the floor. Fred Hollows had seven children. I wonder if they travelled around the world with him. It would take about five minutes to earn a million frequent flyer points if they did. Fred Hollows would have used them to buy medical equipment or something, though. You don't become Australian of the Year by getting yourself a six-hundred litre refrigerator with an ice dispenser.

I read on and discover that you can use your frequent flyer points to donate to the *Fred Hollows Foundation!*

I'm not kidding.

I've never been more impressed by anything in my whole life.

The next morning when I wake early for cross-country training, Dad is already up and ready to leave for work. He looks even more like a spotted tree frog in the semi-darkness – he kind of blends in with his surroundings. Especially out the front where we have lots of small and medium-sized rocks on either side of the path.

After watching us run around the oval, Mr Winsock says to Peta and Ahmed: 'Great work! You two really have what it takes!' To me he says, 'Well done, Jesse. I never thought you'd make it.'

We all head to the canteen for breakfast. Mr S is there, making a coffee in his eco-cup. He makes toast for us with lots of butter – right up to the edges. I only have time to eat half a piece and have a few sips of hot chocolate before the bell goes, though. I don't want to be rushing breakfast just to get to class on time so in future, I'll have to either run a bit faster or only do three laps.

Turns out I didn't need to run anyway because Mrs Leeman isn't in class when I get there. Ms Janik is taking the class by herself, so we work on our projects and talk and have fun like a normal Grade 6 class. The only one not relaxed is Braden. That's because Rey is away today. Every time she is away, he's worried Mrs Leeman is going to move Minha back to her old desk and his holiday in the outback will come to an end.

During recess, I look through our classroom window and Mrs Leeman is in there, sitting at one of the desks up the back. *With Rey.* So she *is* at school. I can't imagine anything worse than private lessons with Mrs Leeman. Or what terrible thing Rey could've done to get punished in this way.

Minha is over in the Preps' veggie garden, rescuing caterpillars before Miss Agostino sprays the leaves with her all-natural-ingredients pest killer. I decide to ask her about Rey.

'Hey, Minha.'

'Hey.'

'Uh … is Rey having lessons with Mrs Leeman? *Extra* ones, I mean?'

'Yeah, I think so,' Minha says, transferring caterpillars into an ice-cream container. 'She misses a lot of school because of her treatment.'

'What kind of treatment?'

Minha pauses with a loaded leaf in each hand and looks at me. 'Why don't you ask her yourself, Jesse?'

As if I'd do *that*. What a ridiculous suggestion.

'She's coming over to my house later on,' Minha continues, 'for dinner. Dad won't mind if you want to come over too.'

'That's okay,' I say, feeling a bit awkward. 'Thanks for the offer, though.'

It's a bit awkward because Minha has a 'pets before people' policy at her house. No one is allowed to have dinner until they've fed all their animals. I know for a fact that Minha has six chickens, three dogs, two cats, eight hermit crabs and a terrapin, which is like a miniature turtle that lives in puddles. I might not *get* any dinner. I hope Rey gets a big lunch at the Children's Centre and isn't allergic to hair or feathers.

At lunchtime, Braden and I wait for Jun outside Mr Winsock's office. Jun is in there trying to persuade him *not* to have a House Cup this year. Meetings in Mr Winsock's office never go for more than five minutes because his office is actually the sports equipment room. It *stinks* in there. You have to run in, get what you want and run out again without taking a breath.

Two minutes later the door opens, and Jun tells us Mr Winsock has given him a lunchtime detention.

'What did you do?' Braden asks as we walk to the retaining wall.

'I didn't *do* anything,' Jun says. 'Mr Winsock said, "You need to find your competitive spirit and spread it around to the other students".'

'And?' I ask.

'And I told him "competitive spirit" sounds like headlice ...'

Jun has to report to the staffroom for detention after he's eaten lunch with us.

At the wall, Wilson Two pokes his head out and pulls Thomas Moore's ham sandwich back into his hole. When he opens his mouth, I see his tongue. It's blue. So his full name is Shingleback Blue-tongue Wilson Two.

* * *

On Friday morning at training, I run two laps easily and then two more not-so-easily. It's solid but I need to run six laps if I'm going to be able to compete in the cross-country. I'm starting to think about cross-country almost as much as breakfast.

Mr Winsock suggests I do some running around at home for extra practice.

'Around where?'

'Anywhere,' he says. 'The garden, to and from school – just incorporate running into your daily routine.'

That's quite a good idea except I already do quite a bit of running at home. I run to the bathroom and back because the heater doesn't make it down that far. And if I'm on the couch and want something from the kitchen, I only have five seconds to run around the corner, get what I want and run back again before the dog takes my spot. I must be going a bit faster though because I have time for two pieces of toast today. Mr S has buttered a whole stack ready for us. I put chocolate powder on mine when no one's looking. If I stand far enough away, it looks like Vegemite.

Around midday, Ms Janik puts some music on while we work on our Great Australians projects. She must think that Mrs Leeman won't be back again today. Normally, Alex and I would muck around until Ms Janik tells us off but today he's working quietly on his bit of the poster as if Mrs Leeman is still in the room.

Before we pack up, we get to see what Ms Kendall's class are working on. I hope no one else is doing an eye surgeon and copies our cataract idea. Peta's group are doing Reverend John Flynn. Their whole project is a giant plane, which makes sense because he started the Royal Flying Doctor Service. But it's only a giant plane – there's no writing on their poster yet. If they were in our class they'd be staying in at lunchtime. Braden and I stop next to the poster about Cathy Freeman, the Olympian. It's pretty good.

I say, 'Do you think if I wrote a letter to Cathy Freeman she might tell me how I can better run the cross-country?'

'I don't know,' Braden says, 'she's kind of busy. See? She has her own Foundation. *Education for Indigenous children*,' he reads off the poster. 'And I think she was more of a *short* distance runner,' he adds. 'Her race was the 400 metres.'

Braden wanders off to look at the other posters.

I don't think it matters that Cathy Freeman's event was the 400 metres. The cross-country is two kilometres. I'll just ask her what to do and then do it five times.

At lunchtime, I put my asparagus and lentil slice on the rock next to Thomas Moore's ham sandwich. Wilson Two pokes his nose out and pulls the sandwich back into his hole. He leaves the slice untouched.

I'm gaining more respect for that lizard every day.

Just before the bell, Ms Janik reminds us that our presentations are next Thursday. Then *after* that, on Friday, they'll be displayed at the Grade 6 graduation assembly.

Mrs Leeman announces that a special guest is coming to graduation assembly to view our projects and choose a winner. She doesn't say who or why. Ms Janik looks as surprised as we are about the special guest. Even when Ms Janik is taking the class, Mrs Leeman is the person actually in charge. Every time she comes up to the front of the classroom, Ms Janik stands to one side as if Mrs Leeman is the prime minister and Ms Janik is only here to drive her to a meeting.

* * *

On Monday, I'm running six laps at training and keeping up with the kids at the back. Peta runs the first two with me then another six and she still finishes first. The only kid who's anywhere near as good as Peta is Ahmed. He confesses to Mr Winsock he's been running around all over the place *out* of school for about two years. Mr Winsock gets all excited and starts talking about inter-school and regionals.

'That's terrific, Ahmed. You and Peta can be here early for training every morning if you like. I wonder if Mrs Overbeek would let us have the gym at lunchtime?'

Ahmed doesn't look all that enthusiastic. Maybe he runs outside of school because he wants to eat lunch at lunchtime.

In the canteen, the parent helper is already there, chatting to Mr S and making the lunch orders. She gives me a vanilla slice when Mr Winsock's not looking. I break it in half and give the other bit to Peta. It seems like the right thing to do. She *did* reunite me with breakfast, after all. And introduce me to the three-kilogram caterer's tin of chocolate powder.

It's a good thing I had the vanilla slice too, because at recess, I discover the contents of my lunch box look as horrible as yesterday's. When the bell rings, Alex doesn't wait for me at our bags as usual, so I go down to the wall with Braden and Peta. Jun has a meeting with Mrs Overbeek about graduation assembly. Alex is already at the wall when we get there, sitting by himself.

I scatter a few pieces of oatmeal cookie on the rock and wait. A few minutes later, Wilson Two inches out of his hole and takes little nibbles from the closest bit, then disappears back into the wall. He's probably waiting for Thomas Moore to turn up with something better. It's so quiet on the wall, I'm relieved when Thomas Moore does appear. But he and Huong don't stay. They break up a choc-chip cookie on the rock then wander off to play under some trees. We sit in silence again until Jun arrives. He seems much happier than after his last meeting with Mrs Overbeek.

'We're going to give the teachers pot plants instead of flowers,' he says, smiling.

'Mrs Overbeek changed her mind? Just like that?' Alex asks, suspiciously. It's the first thing he's said the whole of recess.

'Well ... sort of,' Jun says. 'She said we could give the teachers pot plants as long as she gets to decide which bits of my thank-you speech to leave out.'

He opens his lunch box and starts eating. Jun's vice-captaincy meetings are not so much meetings as negotiations.

We all sit really still and Wilson Two comes right out, grabs a whole piece of choc-chip cookie and eats it right there on the rock.

Thomas Moore will have to stop giving him junk food because he's getting fatter. It won't be from eating any of my lunch.

In the afternoon, we work on our projects for the last time. Everyone agrees I can take our Great Australians poster home to put the finishing touches on it. The only thing left to do is draw coloured borders around the outside and I have a set of seventy-two coloured pencils including twelve metallic ones at home. They're too good to keep at school.

Just before the bell, Mr Winsock comes into our classroom to talk about Athletics Day. Mrs Leeman makes an excuse and leaves the room because she knows how boring the next fifteen minutes are going to be. Mr Winsock gives everyone a program of events. The first thing I notice is the cross-country is 2.4 kilometres. That's a whole *400 metres* more than I'm prepared for! 400 metres is Cathy Freeman's whole race. I bet no one said to her a few days before her event, 'By the way … we've decided to make you run a bit further today – hope you don't mind.' The second thing I notice is that the cross-country is the last event. Now I will have to spend the whole afternoon worrying about it. Mr Winsock finishes up by telling us how much fun Athletics Day is and how we need to be on 'our best behaviour'.

I don't see how we can have fun *and* be on our best behaviour at the same time.

'To get into the spirit of things,' Mr Winsock continues, 'you can wear, just for one day, a T-shirt in the colour of your house.'

Braden raises his hand. 'What if it has writing on it, sir?'

'Well, I suppose that's all right. But no bad words.'

'Is "bum" a bad word, sir?'

Everyone laughs nervously because Mrs Leeman could be back at any minute. We might not have long.

'Yes. You may not wear a shirt with … that word on it.'

'How about "poo"?' Braden asks.

'Or that word.'

'How about "wee"?'

'Yes.'

'So, "bum" and "poo" are bad words but "wee" is okay?' Jun asks.

'What? No. Listen. You may not wear a T-shirt with any words on it. Then there's no confusion. Am I making myself clear?'

Minha raises her hand. 'What about a picture of a bum, sir?'

'Don't be ridiculous. Who has a T-shirt with a picture of a bum on it?'

Five or six hands go up.

Later, I unroll the poster on my desk in front of the fish tank. Einstein is stationed in front of the castle as usual. He looks impressed with our work. There's five big blocks of neat writing about our Great Australian and the middle looks a bit mysterious until you lift the flap and see the eye underneath. I notice that the fish tank is looking a bit mysterious too and realise it's because the castle and treasure chest and stuff are totally green. I should probably clean them now and do the poster's borders a bit later. Or before school tomorrow.

I get the cleaning stuff out of my cupboard and the net to catch the fish.

The little fish go berserk as usual when I put them in the takeaway container. It takes ages to clean everything because I've left it for so long. The castle takes the longest. I find an old toothbrush to get into all the cracks. I'm tempted to use Noah's current toothbrush, but he hasn't been annoying me enough lately to justify it.

By the time I've finished, it's really late. Mum tells me to go to bed, so I plop the fish back into the tank and leave everything on my desk. I can tip out the old fish water and put the cleaning stuff away in the morning.

I have to be up early anyway to finish the poster before school. I remember to set my alarm.

As soon as I wake up, I know something's wrong straightaway. The takeaway container is on my desk, *empty*. There's a crack running all the way across the bottom and water is all over my desk and the floor. The whole area is a marshy bog land of groundwater and underground water. I hold up the poster and the last few drops of water fall off it. Alex and Braden's bits are barely visible – you can only see where their pen has dented the paper. The tracing paper is kind of stuck on now and when I peel it away, the eye is just a swirl of colours.

The Fred Hollows poster is ruined.

And our presentation is in two days' time.

CHAPTER TEN

On the way to school Tuesday morning, I tell Braden about the poster. He stares at me for a really long time but doesn't really say anything. We walk to school in silence where I'm going to have to face Rey, Jun and Alex. Even though Alex and I are hardly talking, I'm dreading telling him the most. I don't know why.

Jun and Alex are on the steps. I take the poster down to the retaining wall. Alex's mouth actually drops open when I unroll it.

'What happened?'

'I left … water got all over it.'

Alex looks at me. He wants to know *how* water got all over it.

'I left a container of water on top of it,' I say. 'Cleaning the fish tank. It must have had a crack in it or something.'

Alex says, 'What are we going to do? Our presentation is on Thursday.'

'I don't know. I'll tell Mrs Leeman it was my fault. Maybe we can—'

'—and what about graduation assembly?'

'I *know*. I'm sorry. I'm sorry, *okay?*'

'Maybe Kade could—'

'Why do you talk about Kade all the time?' I interrupt.

'I don't.'

'You *do*. He's always at your house or you're at his house.' I know I'm being unfair but I can't help it. My mouth is talking without me.

'No, he isn't. We just have to work together and I'm only there on Wednesdays—'

'Yeah, but that doesn't mean—'

'You don't know *anything*.' Alex stands up. 'All your friends are *here*.'

Everyone's quiet then Alex suddenly yells, his voice cracking, 'Everyone thinks I'm so happy and excited, but I'm not! *I'm not!* No one cares what I want to do!' He runs across the courtyard, pushes past the groups of kids standing on the stairs and disappears into the corridor.

Quite a few faces stare after Alex and look back at where he ran from.

After a few minutes, Jun says to me, 'I *like* the poster like this, but you forgot to do the borders.'

'I'm going to look for Rey,' I tell Braden and Jun, but I feel too miserable about what just happened with Alex to actually do anything.

Instead, I walk around the school and head down to where Mr S is sitting by the adventure playground in the duty teacher's vest. He glances over at my crinkly rolled-up poster. 'So, how are things, Jesse?'

'Things are bad.'

Mr S pretends he's watching the kids on the adventure playground and not talking to me. 'Oh? How so?'

A big tear rolls down my face and lands on the Fred Hollows poster. Great. *More* water damage.

'Alex is mad at me about something and I don't know what to do,' I tell him.

Mr S stares into space tapping his chin for so long I think maybe he's forgotten I'm here. Eventually he says, 'I see. That's a tough one, but I've got a couple of things you could have a think about. Ready?'

I nod.

'The first one is, it sounds as though Alex is not so much angry with *you* as worried about something else.'

'… And?'

'And I think you'll find change can be difficult for *everyone*. Alex might be struggling with the idea of going to a different school.'

'What do you mean?' I ask.

'What I mean is that Alex has to make a very tough decision … and he needs his friends more than ever right now. Do you follow?'

'I *think* so.'

Mr S smiles at me then points at the crinkly poster. 'What happened here?'

I tell him about the fish tank water and wrecking our poster and everything.

'Oh, dear. I think you'll have to take that one up with your teacher. I can have a quiet word with Mrs Leeman if you like?'

'Thanks … but I think I want to do it myself.'

Mr S looks pleased and says, 'I know you'll do the right thing, Jesse.'

I'm not sure if he's talking about Alex or the poster. Probably Alex, because that's what Grandpa said too and if Mr S isn't *actually* a grandpa, he's definitely old enough to *be* one.

As we walk to class, he says, 'Do you mind if I ask you a question of my own? How do you think Ian is doing? In his new position, I mean?'

'I think he's doing okay but he doesn't need to be so cheerful all the time,' I reply. 'Like ... talking about stuff isn't always fun so there's no point trying to *make* it fun.'

Mr S laughs. 'Ian is still very young. He'll get there sooner or later.'

I nod, but what is he talking about? I know Ian is twenty-four because he told us. Mr S must be confusing him with one of his other children.

Sitting in class all morning, I still feel terrible. Rey isn't in class today so I can't tell her about the poster. And I should care more about what Braden and Jun think too but I only care that I've made things worse with Alex when things were already bad.

When the bell goes for recess, I wait until everyone else has left the classroom except for me and my friends before I walk up to the front and tell Ms Janik that I wrecked our Great Australians poster. The others stay back with me, but I do all of the talking. I can feel Mrs Leeman gliding up the aisle from the back of the room like a piranha who's spotted some fish looking in the other direction.

Ms Janik looks at our Fred Hollows poster – now dried and crinkly, swirly-coloured and with no writing on it. 'Oh, no! Well, I guess we can … I mean, I'm not sure if it's …' She seems as upset as I am.

Mrs Leeman lifts up the tracing paper cataract and looks at the swirly eye underneath. Then she holds the poster up and examines the back and the front like a detective. 'Come and see me at the end of recess,' she finally says. She rolls up the poster so we all know the subject is closed for now and that we need to go outside or else.

Recess drags for about a hundred years. Peta is talking about stuff, trying to be cheerful, but it's not really working. She's the only one not in Mrs Leeman's class so she doesn't really know how much trouble I will be in. Alex isn't even talking to me. He's not talking to anyone, though, which is something. It's something, but not a *good* something.

Wilson Two comes out and eats some dried apricot out of my dried apricot slice. I wish I could lie around all day not having to worry about anything except food. Apart from maybe eating *too much* food. Wilson Two is getting bigger every day.

We go back to the classroom just before the end of recess. Ms Janik opens the door and Braden, Alex, Jun and I stand in a little semi-circle waiting for Mrs Leeman to say something. She walks around behind her desk and speaks to me as if the others aren't there.

'Jesse, Ms Janik and I have been discussing how difficult it would have been for you to bring this to the attention of your group.' Then, to all of us: 'Give your workbooks to me so I can see what was on the poster.' We scramble to our desks and leave our books in a sad pile. Mrs Leeman picks them up.

'All right, then. Leave it with me,' she says.

I look back at the others. Mrs Leeman is wearing her 'subject closed' expression. I'm either not in any trouble or in so *much* trouble Mrs Leeman needs more time to think of a punishment. I can't think of a punishment that will make me feel any worse than I already feel. The four of us walk to the door in silence. Ms Janik hasn't said anything the whole time either.

Opening the door for us is her only contribution to the whole exchange.

I get up early the next morning for training, keep up with Peta for two whole laps and run four more. I'm the last one to finish and I don't even care. After training, there's two sandwich loaves and the caterer's tin of hot chocolate powder but I'm not hungry so I take my toast down to the retaining wall. Wilson Two is already out sunning himself on the rock. He's huge now. He has to reverse into his hole with his bit of toast like a delivery van. I shouldn't have put so much chocolate powder on it.

At recess, Jun describes the final meeting he and Samra had with Mr Winsock about the House Cup.

'I told Mr Winsock I do believe in competition,' Jun says to us, 'just not with each other.'

Peta frowns. 'But what about if you come first? Isn't that good?'

'It's okay,' Jun says, 'but it's not *important*. The person who wins is faster, not better.' He unwraps his recess and arranges it on his lunch box lid.

We are all quiet.

Finally, Braden says, 'What did Mr Winsock say?'

'He said it doesn't matter if you don't come first as long as you're *trying* to come first.'

As soon as we come in after recess, the intercom from the office beeps. It must be Miss Creighton on the other end because the conversation goes for about three seconds and then Mrs Leeman bangs the receiver back on the wall and tells me to get my stuff together because I'm leaving early. She doesn't say why. Just my luck I'm too upset about the poster and Alex to fully appreciate it. Up at the office though, Mum is telling Miss Creighton that Dad's had an accident on his bike and broken his wrist.

'The van just came out of nowhere, and on the wrong side of the road,' Mum is saying.

'The same thing happened to my brother,' Miss Creighton says, 'only he broke his leg in three places.' She says it as if there's a House Cup presented for bone breaking.

Mum steers me towards the office door. 'Hurry up, Jesse. I want to get back to the hospital.' I scramble into the car, which is in the teachers' carpark.

We drive in silence.

When we arrive at the hospital, Mum turns straight into the visitor carpark without even looking for a spot on the street! If Dad finds out we're paying eleven dollars an hour to park the car, he might need to stay in hospital even longer.

As we get a ticket out of the machine, I ask Mum, 'Where is Noah?'

'Noah's going to stay at Bree's after school.'

'Why can't I go to Alex's? Or Braden's?'

'Because you're here with me, Jesse.'

That doesn't really answer my question, but I get the feeling Mum doesn't want to discuss it right now.

In the Emergency Department, we tell the nurse behind the glass window with the holes in it that we're here to see Dad and he unlocks the door for us. The people in the waiting room are probably jealous that we can walk right in while they have to stay there watching the miniature TV on full volume for a hundred more hours.

Dad is in cubicle seventeen, right down the end. I'm relieved to see he looks okay except for a big graze on his forehead and his right wrist and hand, which is swollen and bruised. It's resting on a thick plastic tray and has its own pillow. Dad's wearing a white hospital gown that isn't done up at the back so I make sure I stay standing in front of him. Underneath his bed, there's a yellow bag marked 'patient's clothing'. Even through the plastic I can see his spotted tree frog suit. I wonder if they had to cut it off him like they do on TV. Dad tries to sit up when he sees me, but Mum tells him to lie down in a bossy voice as if it's me or Noah in the bed.

'Have you been X-rayed yet? Did they give you something for the pain?' Mum asks, looking at his purple fingers.

'I have to be seen by orthopaedics,' Dad says in a weird scratchy voice. 'They're hoping to do it tonight.'

Do what tonight? I thought orthopaedics were the things Grandpa put in his shoes.

'But I did get something for the pain,' Dad whispers to Mum. He rests his head back on the pillow. His face has gone all shiny with sweat even though he's not doing anything.

The guy from the opposite cubicle comes in and introduces himself as 'Ani' like we're at a New Year's Eve barbeque and not hospital. He has a big graze on his jaw and there are a few teeth missing on the bottom. It looks like someone has punched him in the face. He smiles. 'This is my third time in the hospital this year.' Then he looks at the graze on Dad's head and tells him off for wearing the wrong bike helmet! Maybe someone *has* punched him in the face.

It makes me feel all shaky when I hear Ani talk about Dad's bike helmet. I try not to think about what could've happened if he hadn't been wearing it.

Ani starts talking to Dad about heart rates and speedometers. The nurses have locked their watches in the medicine cupboard because the alarms and sensors were interfering with the medical equipment. According to the beeps coming from the cupboard, Dad and Ani are both behind in their step count and their heart rates are not where they should be – in the red zone. I get the impression the watches might have put some *other* patients' hearts in the red zone though.

Dad croaks to Ani, 'I can't believe my bike is totalled ... there's two K I'll never see again.'

Dad's bike cost *two thousand* dollars? Two thousand! We don't need to worry about where we park the car, then. If I had two thousand dollars, I would buy a Maremma sheepdog and a pair of noise-cancelling headphones. Or fifteen hundred chocolate beetles. I wouldn't buy a *bike*.

It's so boring waiting for the doctor to come back. Mum gets sick of me complaining and gives me some money for the vending machine. She tells me not to bring any food back here – Dad isn't allowed anything to eat or drink because he'll be having an operation tonight. I wasn't planning to bring anything back anyway. This whole Emergency Department smells like a swimming pool toilet block.

Things are a bit more interesting in the corridor. Two police officers are talking to a guy in a courier uniform. He has a few stitches on his head. Maybe they're about to arrest him because he's getting really upset, yelling and waving his arms around.

'I don't *know* where he came from! He came out of thin air! How about asking *him* why he was on the wrong side of the road? How about that?'

The cop reaches behind her back and I think she's going for her handcuffs or something, but she brings out a few coins.

'Okay, mate … settle down. Let's grab a coffee and get it together before we talk. All right?'

The two cops walk down the corridor with the courier guy unrestrained.

I can't find a vending machine anywhere in the hospital. Confusing arrows in the corridors direct me towards a kiosk in the foyer that only has soft toys, magazines and balloons in it. On the other side of the foyer it looks like they're setting up for a party or something. Two long tables are on either side of the automatic doors. One of them has a million glasses on it and the other one has cups, saucers and a big stack of Westmoore Hospital serviettes. A group of people in suits are having a discussion about miniature pastries so I look around for a third table but there isn't one, or any *actual* pastries. While I'm standing there, an old lady sitting in the corner says something and all the people in suits nod and move the tables along a bit. She must be like the Mrs Leeman of the hospital.

I'm about to leave when I hear a voice from the corner. 'Hey, Jesse!'

I look over and see Rey and another girl sitting at a little table with a whole bunch of books and stuff in front of them.

'This is Mari,' Rey says, nodding towards the other girl, 'from my old school. Jesse's from my new school,' she explains to Mari.

'What's going on here?' I ask Rey, pointing to the people in suits.

'It's for the opening of the new Children's Centre,' Rey says, 'on Friday night.'

'Yeah,' Mari says really quietly. She gestures towards the corner. 'That lady is a Westmoore …'

'Like the school?'

'Like the *hospital*,' Mari says in a normal voice, laughing. She packs up half the books on the table. 'I'll see you upstairs, Rey. Chips, no salt?'

'Yep. No salt,' Rey agrees as Mari leaves, then she turns to me. 'Sorry. I didn't ask you why you're here?'

'It's my dad,' I tell her. 'He was hit by a van.'

'*Oh, no!* Is he going to be okay?'

'Yeah. But his wrist is broken and his bike is totally wrecked.'

Rey giggles.

'What?' I say.

'I'm sorry. It's not funny. It just sounds like you're more worried about the bike than your dad.'

I start laughing too. 'I know … I'm not, though. It's weird seeing him down there. It makes me feel sick or something.'

Rey nods. 'I know. I still get scared sometimes, even though I'm here all the time.'

'Oh. So, why *are* you here all the time?' I ask her.

'Well. I was sick last year and now my kidneys don't work properly,' Rey explains. 'So I have to get connected to a machine.'

'Like a kidney machine?' I picture something like a copy machine in the shape of Alex's swimming pool.

'Yeah … but it's *that* big,' Rey points to the drinks fridge in the kiosk, 'and it takes hours.'

'Oh.'

'It's not so bad,' Rey continues. 'Mari comes in and we do our homework together. And I have lots of other friends who take it in turns so Mum gets a break, too.'

'You still have friends from your old school?'

'Yeah, heaps. Mari and I have been friends since Prep.'

'Like me and Alex,' I say, thinking.

Neither of us says anything for a while. Then I tell Rey, 'I have to go back to the Emergency Department before they take Dad upstairs.'

'Okay.'

I turn to leave, then remember. 'I have to tell you something … about our Great Australians poster.'

Rey waves her hand at me. 'I know. Mrs Leeman told me.' Then, after a minute, she says, 'Mrs Leeman's a really nice teacher, don't you think?'

I can feel myself going red because it must be a joke, but I don't get it.

'Uh, well … I better go,' I say.

'Try not to worry about your dad too much,' Rey says. 'He'll be okay.'

'I'll try.' Then I add, 'If you want, I could do some

homework with you to keep you company one day. If I did any, I mean.'

Rey laughs because she thinks *that* is a joke. 'Yeah, that would be good. I'll be here.'

Back in the Emergency Department, Ani is sitting on a chair in Dad's cubicle. A nurse comes in and tells him to go back to his *own* cubicle. Ani just laughs and says, 'Okay, Jase. Whatever you say.'

Okay, Jase? Does Ani live here?

Jase pushes the chairs back and ushers in a whole bunch of people. They all crowd into the tiny space around Dad's bed. One of them is wearing a suit and tie so he must not do any messy stuff. He doesn't have a name badge either so he has to introduce himself: Dr Subra from Orthopaedics. All the others listen as if he's about to make an important announcement. I notice Ani has left the cubicle.

'Andrew has a very tricky break in his wrist,' Dr Subra explains to Mum and Dad, 'and he needs an operation to fix it.' The doctor draws quite a bad picture on the back of Dad's blank menu card to show him what he's going to do. I hope he does the operation better than the drawing. The other people in the room look a bit disappointed if you ask me. They were probably hoping for something a bit more technical than 'tricky' and 'fix it'.

Everyone leaves except Jase. He starts getting Dad ready for surgery. 'After your op,' Jase says to Dad, 'they'll take you upstairs for the night. You won't need to come back here again. Lucky you!' Jase checks all of Dad's tubes and rearranges the pillows gently around his broken wrist. He washes the blood off Dad's face with a cloth, then hands a clean one to Mum.

'Pain? Pee? Puke?' he asks Dad, before leaving the cubicle.

'No, no and no,' Dad says, trying to smile. 'But Jase?'

'Yes?'

'Thank you.'

I want to say something to Jase too, but he's already down the other end of the cubicles telling Ani that patients aren't allowed to touch the equipment trolleys. I want to thank Jase for everything he did for us. I only just realised what he *did* do, now that he's not here, and everything's weird and scary again.

We don't leave the hospital until after midnight. On the way home, Mum stops the car at Bree's house to pick up Noah. He jumps in the back, then noticing the front seat is empty, leans over to me.

'Where's Dad?' he whispers.

'In hospital. Where did you think he was?'

'I thought he only broke his wrist.'

'He *did* break his wrist,' I tell Noah. 'That's what he had the operation for.'

I feel bad when Noah's face turns pale. He shifts around to look out of his window, even though it's too dark to see anything. I lean against my own window. I've been thinking very recently that I might like to be a doctor one day. Learning about injuries and how to fix them is quite interesting – it's only looking at them on actual people that I find a bit yucky.

We drive on in silence for a few minutes.

'Okay, boys,' Mum says while the car's stopped at a traffic light. 'Now that you're both here … Dad and I have been talking.'

Noah turns to me but I'm as puzzled as he is.

'We've decided to rethink the healthy eating regime and go back to the way things were,' Mum announces. 'More or less.'

The traffic light turns green.

'I still think it's important to eat nutritious food,' Mum continues, 'but perhaps we'll ease up on the less appetising elements of the healthy diet. Dad and I feel it's not … *sustainable.*'

Not sustainable. That's just a fancy way of saying the diet was gross and we all hated it. I think about it: no more birdseed bread, no more carpet tile-wiches, no more breakfast flakes in watery almond milk.

'What about the vitamin pill submarines?' I ask, warily.

'No more vitamin pills,' Mum says. 'I was a bit disappointed in those anyway. Some of them looked a bit soggy and weird.'

Noah and I exchange a glance. His face is looking a lot better now.

'Also, I have a tiny confession to make,' Mum adds. 'I've been cheating a bit.' She keeps her eyes on the road as we turn into our street. 'I hid some chocolate bars in the linen cupboard.'

CHAPTER ELEVEN

Today is presentation day. As soon as I get to school, I'm going to talk to Alex. It's weird being worried about talking to my best friend but not as weird as not talking to him *at all*.

Walking towards the school, I see everyone in their sports uniform and different coloured T-shirts. I've had so many new worries about Dad and Alex and our project, I'd completely forgotten about my *long*-term worries – like Athletics Day. Luckily, I haven't taken my sports uniform home to be washed for about a month (another long-term worry) so it'll still be in my locker. I just won't have a coloured T-shirt.

Thomas Moore is standing at the gate, counting everyone as they arrive.

'You're number forty-two,' he says to me.

'Have you seen Alex? Is he here yet?' I ask him.

'He's here but I can't remember what number he is.'

'That's okay. I've got some important stuff to talk about with him.'

'I've got some important stuff to talk about with him too,' Thomas Moore says.

'By myself, I mean.'

Thomas Moore says, 'Okay,' and follows me anyway.

I find Alex sitting by himself on the retaining wall. I'm a little encouraged when he looks up and sort of smiles.

I wish Thomas Moore would go away but I've been wishing for that since February. Maybe part of finally doing the right thing is letting him come with me.

'Are you still angry?' I ask Alex before I sit down.

'No.'

'I get it if you are.'

'I'm not.'

We sit there for a bit.

'I'm sorry I wrecked our poster,' I say to him.

'Our poster? Oh. That's okay.'

'Also, if you want to go to St Bennett's that's okay, too. I mean I'll miss you, but if you want to go—'

'—I really don't want to go.'

'I don't want to go either,' Thomas Moore says.

Alex says, 'I know I'm supposed to be excited and happy and everything, but I want to be at school with my friends next year … not with a bunch of kids I don't know. It's just that Mum and Dad have told everyone I'm going to St Bennett's so if I *don't* go everyone will be disappointed in me and I'll be letting *everyone* down and I don't know what to do.'

It's the most I've heard him say at once for a while.

'Is that the only reason you don't want to go?' I ask Alex. 'Because the rest of us won't be there?'

Alex shrugs. 'Kind of.'

'So you kind of want to go?'

'Maybe. I don't know,' Alex says, miserably.

'You could talk to Mr S about it,' I suggest.

'Ian says I should tell my Mum and Dad how I feel.'

Oh, yeah. Ian.

'I think you should,' Thomas Moore says.

'Should what?' Alex and I both say together.

'Do what Ian says,' Thomas Moore says. '*Bite the bullet.*'

Alex giggles.

'Yeah!' I agree. '*Get it out in the open … spill the beans.*'

'*Talk it through*,' Alex adds and we both start laughing.

Alex and I watch Thomas Moore run up to the playground.

'If you want to go to St Bennett's, that's okay,' I say again. 'We can still hang out after school and on weekends.'

'And holidays and public holidays and curriculum days,' Alex says.

I say, 'It's a pity I'm not as smart as you – then we could both go.'

'You *are* smart,' Alex says, sounding surprised.

'I'm still on level five Mathletics,' I tell him.

'Yeah, but you have good ideas,' he insists.

'What do you mean?'

'Okay. Like thinking of all those ways to get normal stuff to eat … and putting the vitamin pills back in the bottle. That's smart.'

'Oh, yeah,' I say, slowly.

'And helping Thomas Moore make his own friends before we all go off to high school. I didn't think of that.'

I hadn't thought about those things as being smart before.

'Anyway,' Alex says, 'if I was so smart I'd talk to my

parents about St Bennett's the way you talked to Mrs Leeman about our Great Australians poster.'

'I *had* to do that,' I say, 'because I'm the one who wrecked it.'

'You told her, though. No one made you.'

'I did think about burying it and moving to Antarctica.'

'Yeah, but you didn't,' Alex says.

'I felt like it.'

'Yeah, but you didn't,' he says again, and I don't argue.

After the morning bell rings, instead of doing normal work, Ms Kendall's Grade 6 class brings their Great Australians projects into our classroom. Ms Janik stands up the front and claps her hands together.

'Okay, everyone. Listen up! I want you to push all the desks and chairs to the side ... we need a big space in the middle for the presentations!' All of us in Mrs Leeman's class are too scared to push anything anywhere until Ms Janik assures us she has permission. Even so, we lift the chair legs up so they don't make scrapey noises on the floor.

'What order are we going in?' Jun asks Ms Janik. '*Most* great to *least* great? Or the other way around?'

'You're presenting in alphabetical order,' Mrs Leeman says, writing all the names of the Great Australians on the interactive whiteboard. Our group is about halfway, between Cathy Freeman and Sir John Monash.

Minha's group stands up anxiously. They bring their Sir Donald Bradman poster into the centre of the room and the presentations begin.

All of the projects are really good. When it's our turn, I feel bad all over again that our group doesn't have a poster and that it's no one's fault but mine. We're told to read to the class out of our workbooks, which Mrs Leeman takes out of a big envelope marked 'copy' for some reason.

'Rey is away today, working on the poster for this group,' Mrs Leeman announces before we start. Everyone in the room nods while Alex, Jun, Braden and I try to look as if we knew this bit of information already.

Right when Jun is explaining the eye-slicing part of cataract surgery, the classroom door opens and Mrs Overbeek and Ian tiptoe into the room. Mrs Overbeek must be checking to make sure there are enough posters for tomorrow's assembly. I don't know why Ian's here. He keeps whispering stuff really loudly to Ms Janik over the stacked-up pile of desks. He should be looking out for his *own* wellbeing because Mrs Leeman keeps glancing over in his direction.

After the presentations are over, we're all so relieved it's not funny. Ms Janik collects everyone's posters and says, 'Well done, well done' about four million times, even to our group, which doesn't have a poster.

Down at the retaining wall at recess, Wilson Two is lying stretched out on the rock in the sun. He doesn't want anything we offer him to eat. I hope he's not waiting for a sandwich because we'll only be around for recess today. When the bell goes, everyone from Prep to Grade 6 will walk down to Young's Sports Centre for Athletics Day.

'Why don't you have a coloured T-shirt?' Braden asks me.

'I forgot ... what with Dad and everything.'

'I might have a spare one,' Peta says, 'from training.' We all go with Peta and find a green T-shirt with an emu on it that fits me okay. Thinking about training makes me start worrying about the cross-country again. It just slides right into the worry zone recently vacated by the Great Australians presentations.

When the time comes, Miss Agostino, Mr S and Ian walk to the sports centre with us. On the way, Mr Wilson drives past in his car. Some kids start yelling, 'Hey, Mr Wilson! Mr Wilson! Give us a lift!' until

Mr S says, 'Anyone yelling has to carry the equipment bag.' He's smiling though and gives the bag to Ian. When we get to the road opposite the park, Miss Agostino makes us cross in a big clump, like sheep. A lady stops her car to give way to us and she starts laughing because there's so many of us. She has to wait for about fifty hours.

The first part of Athletics Day is a bit boring. The same four or five kids win every event. Peta wins everything in her category and Ahmed wins everything in his. Ahmed should tell Mr Winsock *now* that he's thinking about starting a dog-walking business over the summer holidays or something and won't be available for any training next year. Otherwise he'll be made to volunteer for everything.

We all have to stay in the outside area of the sports centre unless we want to go to the toilet or the kiosk.

At lunchtime I ask Alex, 'How much money do *you* have?'

'Same as you,' he says, looking. We decide to combine our money because everything at the kiosk is really expensive. We buy a box of hot chips and a cheese and tomato sandwich. Without putting our money together, it's a sandwich *or* chips.

Ms Kendall's brought a massive bag of chocolate reindeers – enough for about four per kid. Three days ago the sight of a bag like that would have given me a dizzy spell.

The last race before the cross-country is the three-legged teachers' race. Samra pulls all the names out of an ice-cream container and Jun ties the teachers' ankles together with coloured ties. Mr Winsock has been teamed up with Miss Agostino. I can tell he's disappointed because Miss Agostino thinks the three-legged race is a joke.

All the pairs line up at the start line and Samra yells, *'Ready, set, go!'*

Miss Agostino falls over after about two minutes. Mr S and Mrs Hillman the librarian stop to help, which is not easy because they have to go together, in the same direction. Mr Wilson starts yelling for the First Aid Officer, which causes bit of confusion because Miss Agostino *is* the First Aid Officer and has the only key to the first-aid cupboard. Eventually Mr S unties his ankle and gets some frozen peas for Miss Agostino and elevates her ankle, which is now puffy and swollen. Mr S does a lot for someone who has retired. Maybe Ian's *real* job is to replace Mr S when he actually leaves.

I'm hoping that Mr Winsock has forgotten about the cross-country and we can all go back to school early, but he's found the megaphone. 'All long-distance competitors are to meet at the starting line,' he announces.

Peta and I walk over to the red line.

So do about twenty other kids!

We're literally about to start the race when I find out that during this term, there's been training *after school* as well. And after-school food is better than breakfast food!

How am I supposed to run when I've just discovered I got up early every Monday, Wednesday and Friday for a whole term unnecessarily?

Mr Winsock says, 'Ready, set, go!' and we all jog forwards on the track. That's how you do it in cross-country running. If you're too fast at the start, you'll never be able to do the whole thing.

As soon as we're off the track, though, Peta, Ahmed and half the others disappear into the trees. When I make it past the first checkpoint, Alex and Braden are there, yelling, '*C'mon, Jesse! Go!*'

They must have run faster than me to get to the checkpoint first. It's much harder running around trees and logs and over sticks than it is running around the oval. After a while, every log I see looks like one of those armchairs that tilt back so you can lie down.

I can't see anyone, now. Maybe I passed them all in the bushy bit in the middle.

Every five years or so, I run past a red checkpoint flag.

My lungs are starting to feel like sandwich bags full of cement.

I'm so tired.

It feels like I'm the only one out here.

Funny, it's quite peaceful in the park on my own. It's so quiet away from the kids and the road and Mr Winsock yelling stuff through the megaphone. I wish cross-country could be done in two parts so you could sit down and have a rest at the halfway mark.

Just when I think my legs are going to fold up like a trestle table, I see the trail. Alex, Braden and Jun are jumping around, cheering. Lots of kids are jumping around, cheering. I summon the strength of a hundred Great Australians to sprint the last little bit, cross the finish line and flop down in the grassy centre of the track.

CHAPTER TWELVE

'**D**id I win?' I croak.

'Did you win what?' Peta says, looking down at me collapsed on the grass. She's eating an icy pole.

'Did I win the *race*? The cross-country?'

'Oh. No. I won it about half an hour ago.' Peta giggles. 'You came last.'

Alex is busy calculating something on a map of the park.

'You ran 4.1 kilometres,' he says.

'What? I did?'

'Yeah, see?' He shows me the map. 'You were supposed to run to the left of the flags, but you went to the right, which took you all the way up here and across the top and down. So it was 4.1 kilometres.'

I can't believe I ran 4.1 kilometres! That's further than I've ever run before.

'You ran almost twice the length of the race!' Alex says. 'That's amazing! You're fantastic!'

And I finally understand what Jun has been trying to say all along … because running 4.1 kilometres doesn't feel like last to me; it feels better than coming first.

I recover enough to stand up and sit with my friends in the shade. After a few minutes, Thomas Moore drags his stuff over to us.

'My nanna's coming to the assembly tomorrow,' he says, sitting next to me.

'Lots of people are coming to the assembly tomorrow,' Jun says. 'It's graduation.'

Thomas Moore shakes his head. 'She's the special guest.'

'She can't be,' Braden says. 'The special guest is a well-known person. Someone everyone knows.'

'It's my nanna,' Thomas Moore says, standing up and handing me the school newsletter.

'Actually,' I say, looking at the newsletter, 'the special guest is someone called Deandra Moore. We should look it up.'

'I *am* looking it up,' Peta says, staring at her phone. 'Here. Listen. *Phillip and India Westmoore, began Westmoore Foundation in 1956, donating their entire estate and proceeds to the provision of education and health care for marginalised communities. The local hospital and primary school still bear their original surname. They later shortened their surname to Moore.*' Peta glances up from her reading. 'Westmoore Primary!' She continues, '*Their daughter in-law, Deandra Moore, manages the Foundation and enjoys spending time with her grandson, Thomas!*'

We all turn to Thomas Moore. He grins at us.

I lean forwards and look at the picture on Peta's phone. It's the lady from the hospital foyer.

Mr Winsock's voice rings out through the megaphone: 'Okay, everyone! If you could all get into your House groups … we'll have the House Cup presentation! Please come up here, Samra and Junli.'

We all stand up noisily and shuffle around for ages. Everyone's giggling and whispering.

Mr Winsock leans towards the megaphone again. 'I believe I said, *in your House groups* … Team colours, please!'

'They *are* in their House groups,' Jun says, smiling. He's wearing a multi-coloured shirt.

Mr Winsock looks confused because every House is a jumble of colours. We're in our House groups but no one's wearing the right coloured shirt. Mr S and Ian have multi-coloured shirts, too, except they can do what they like because Mr S is retired and Ian makes up his own rules.

Mr Wilson steps forwards. 'Let's get on with it, shall we, Mr Winsock?'

'Er, yes,' Mr Winsock says, looking a bit deflated. 'Our school captain Samra Boulos and vice-captain Junli Zhao will now read out a few highlights from today, then present the winners' cup to the House captains.'

Samra and Jun walk up and take the megaphone from Mr Wilson.

Samra starts: 'Hannah L in Grade 4 ran one hundred metres in fifteen seconds!' Everyone laughs because her voice sounds so funny through the megaphone.

'Huong P in Prep found an echidna in the carpark,' Jun adds. His voice sounds even funnier.

'Ahmed K in Grade 4 jumped 2.9 metres in long jump!' Samra says.

Everyone claps for Ahmed but we're all rolling around on the grass laughing at the megaphone and the

T-shirts and because it's the second-last day of school and everything's funny.

Jun yells into the megaphone, 'Mr Wilson got fined $125 for parking in a loading zone.'

Mr Winsock takes the megaphone from Jun. 'All right, Junli. That's enough highlights.' He announces that Gold is the winner of the House Cup but it's hard to hear what he's saying because we're all talking and laughing. The Gold House captains step forwards (in green and red T-shirts) and invite the other House captains to join them up the front to collect the cup, which has *all* the coloured ribbons tied onto it.

We pack up our stuff and walk back to school with Mr S and Ian. It's a lot further than it was on the way, especially for me because I've just run 4.1 kilometres. I notice Ian's not carrying the equipment now. It's probably in Mr Wilson's car.

Back at school, we've still got a few minutes to wait before the final bell rings.

'Let's see if Wilson Two is out,' Alex says. 'We only have today and tomorrow to see him.'

The others don't want to come, so just me and Alex head down to the wall. Wilson Two is still lying on the rock in the sun. His belly is huge – like a big lizard-skin football.

'Wow,' Alex says. 'Look how fat he is.'

'I know. We shouldn't give him biscuits and stuff. Too many carbohydrates.'

'Listen to you – *carbohydrates*,' Alex says, laughing. 'You stopped that diet just in time.'

'I *know*!'

The next morning when Braden and I get to school, Alex is waiting at the gate. Something must have happened because he's smiling and jumping around. He wants to wait until Jun and Peta arrive before he says anything. When they do, we all go down to the retaining wall even though the first bell has rung and we have less than five minutes. Thomas Moore and Huong are already there, collecting beetles in Huong's sunhat.

Everyone looks at Alex, waiting for him to say something.

'I talked to my parents,' he announces, 'about next year.'

'About time,' Peta says.

'What did you say?' I ask him. 'What did *they* say?'

'It was really good,' Alex says. 'I told them everything … about St Bennett's and how I'm scared to go.' He pauses for a moment. 'They were happy I told them, and relieved … because they said I've been really quiet lately.'

'How do they *know* you've been quiet, though?' Braden asks. 'You don't have any brothers or sisters.'

'Yeah, but I talk to *them*,' Alex says, laughing now. 'Anyway, I kind of explained that I didn't say something earlier because I didn't want to disappoint them.'

'And?' Jun says.

'And they said, "You could never disappoint us".'

'*Never?*' Peta says.

'So … you're coming to school with us next year,' I say.

Alex shakes his head. 'No. I'm going to St Bennett's.'

Everyone is quiet.

Alex takes a big breath. 'We talked about everything,' he says. 'What kind of programs they have there and stuff I can do—'

'—I think it's really cool you're going,' Peta breaks in.

'Me too,' I say.

'Really?' Alex looks at me.

'Yep,' I say. 'It really is.'

Alex smiles and drops his shoulders.

'I thought everyone could come around to my house for a swim after graduation tomorrow,' he says. 'Kade really wants to meet all my friends.'

'He does?' I ask.

'Yeah. He's the only one at St Bennett's from his primary school, too,' Alex explains. 'We kind of had no one, together.'

I've been so worried about losing Alex, I never thought about *him* losing *me*. Or that Kade is just a regular kid who wants to eat lunch with someone.

I wonder who will be sitting next to *me* eating lunch next year. It won't be the person sitting next to me *now* – Thomas Moore.

Jun, Peta and Braden wander up when the bell rings, but Alex and I sit there for a while. Thomas Moore jumps down and stands in front of us. 'The bell's gone,' he says. 'You should be in class.'

'Why aren't you in class, then?' Alex asks.

'I'm walking up with you,' he says, looking at us.

'Hey, Alex,' I say, jumping off the wall. 'Ian was right! Saying you should talk to your parents, I mean.'

Alex smiles. 'Yeah, I know.'

'Looks like he *really got through to you*,' Thomas Moore yells and runs off.

When we get to our classroom, Mrs Leeman is busy telling everyone to tidy up and empty their desks. She sends Alex up to the office with the assembly programs. She must be preoccupied because she lets me go with him.

As soon as we walk through the office door, we run into three massive display screens on wheels. Peta, Samra and Rey are pinning all the Great Australians posters onto them. Rey is pinning our Fred Hollows poster onto one of the screens. All the writing has been redone and the eye is fixed. It looks amazing.

'Oh, wow!' I say to Rey. 'You did the *whole* poster again?'

'Yeah,' she says. 'Mrs Leeman made copies of the workbook notes for me.'

'Why did you do it?' I ask. '*You* didn't wreck it, *I* did.'

Rey smiles. 'I know, but it's my poster too and I didn't do a lot to start with—'

Rey is interrupted by Miss Creighton's voice coming from behind the screens: 'Alex! Jesse! Give me those programs and go back to class!' Miss Creighton must have X-ray vision. Alex reaches around the screen, drops the programs and we both run out of the office.

Later that day, in the gym, everyone is talking and laughing because it's the last assembly before holidays. The three display screens from the office are lined up at the back of the stage. It's kind of chaotic until Mrs Leeman walks into the gym and everyone falls silent and gets into their class areas immediately. She can't make the parents be quiet, though. Except for the ones that had her as their teacher fifty years ago.

Deandra Moore is sitting next to Mr Wilson near the stage. He keeps leaning over and talking to her. It *looks* as if he's explaining what's going on. I can tell she's finding him annoying from here. She can *see* what's going on.

Mrs Overbeek starts the assembly by rambling for hours about all the stuff we've done this year. I don't know why. We already know what we've done and the parents can't do anything about it now. Finally, she asks Jun and Samra to 'prepare the presentations', which means push the three portable display screens forwards a bit. Mrs Overbeek waits for a dramatic pause then introduces Thomas Moore's grandmother.

'We have a very special guest with us today for graduation assembly – an exceptional member of our community,' she says, then tells everyone about Deandra Moore and the Moore Foundation.

Alex is making me laugh because he's going '*moop*' under his breath every time Mrs Overbeek says 'exceptional'.

'... the Community Health Centre provides exceptional care to residents ...'

Moop.

'... so that brings us to the new Children's Centre at Westmoore Hospital, where the care is already exceptional ...'

Moop.

'... and will see an expansion of beds and exceptional facilities to care for children and their families.'

Moop.

'... and she is also a grandparent in our school community!' Mrs Overbeek finishes and steps aside.

A voice from the front yells out, 'Hi, Nanna! *Nanna! I'm over here!*'

Deandra Moore stands up and waves to Thomas Moore on her way up to the stage.

I notice some of the teachers and parents stand as well as clap as she walks onto the stage. I'm not expecting my Mum and Dad because Dad is still in hospital so I can't believe it when I see Grandpa and Grandma in the front row! I hope they drove here in Grandma's car.

'Thank you, Mrs Overbeek,' Deandra Moore says, taking the microphone. 'What a privilege it is to be here at your final assembly for the year. I'll come straight to the reason for my visit because I'm sure you're all bursting to get out of here and start your summer holidays.'

Everyone giggles when she says that.

'I understand Grade 6 has been busy all term working together in groups on their Great Australians projects.' She looks around. 'If the school captains could bring them forwards a little so everyone can see them ...' Jun and Samra push the screens right up to the front.

'We can all learn a great deal from the actions of these exceptional people,' Deandra Moore says. 'They all brought and continue to bring about change for the better. I'm supposed to choose the best poster today for the opening of the Children's Centre, but they're *all* terrific ... so I think we can find room in the hospital foyer for every single one of them.'

The hospital foyer! Everyone's really excited – our posters are going to be displayed to the public! Dad will see my project after all.

Deandra Moore continues, 'I think it's very important that the children who visit the centre know what I'm about to tell you now: very few people start exceptional. Something very small has the potential to make a difference. Try to remember that, Grade 6, as you make your way forwards to the next step in your wonderful lives.'

Thomas Moore's nanna walks off the stage and takes her seat. Everyone claps and cheers for ages. I realise Alex didn't 'moop' once, the whole time Deandra Moore was speaking. Next, Jun and Samra bring a little table onto the stage with some pot plants and presents on it. My friends and I already know that the plants are for Ms Kendall and Mrs Leeman. One of the presents on the table is for Ms Janik.

The other is for Ian, who blushes bright red. 'I'm *blown away* by the support I've received at Westmoore Primary,' he says. 'I just hope to be *one of the team* for many years to come.' Alex and I have to laugh twice as hard as usual because this could be our last opportunity.

For the rest of assembly, all the Grade 6s get up on the stage. We play some music we picked out earlier and show some photos on the overhead screen from when we were little. It's funny seeing pictures of us in Prep. We look like babies. It's weird to think of Thomas Moore being up here in six years' time staring at photos of *his* class.

Everyone claps when we leave the gym. Grade 6 go out first and the teachers put the chairs away for us! Alex, Jun, Braden, Peta and I grab our bags and meet down at the retaining wall one last time.

There's already a big crowd at one end of the wall. A whole lot of kids, from all the grades. Thomas Moore is crouching down by the rock; his mouth open in a big soundless 'O' of surprise. Sometime during graduation assembly, Wilson Two has become Wilsons Two to Seventeen. Or maybe Eighteen – the baby ones keep moving around and are difficult to count. They're climbing all over the rock and the wall and all over us if we sit really still.

'That's why she was getting bigger!' Alex says, laughing. Wilson Two looks happy with her family. She's lying half out of her hole on the rock, resting her head on her favourite carbohydrate – a ham sandwich from Thomas Moore's lunch box. She's magically deflated now that she's had her babies. We sit on the wall, letting the baby lizards run up and down our arms. One more day and we would've missed it because Grade 6 is over. *Primary school* is over. No more Mrs Leeman!

I think about Mrs Leeman making us work so hard. Do everything ourselves. Be on time. I think about her giving Rey extra lessons … not telling the class what happened to our poster …

'Hang on … I just need to do something.' I jump off the retaining wall and race up to the staffroom.

Mr S directs me towards the playground where Mrs Leeman is helping some Preps down the slide.

She sees me standing there.

'Jesse? Is everything all right?'

'Mrs Leeman? Um … I just wanted to say … thank you.'

Mrs Leeman smiles and gives me a quick hug. 'You're welcome. Now off you go and enjoy your holidays.'

'You too, Mrs Leeman!' I shout as I run back to join my friends on the retaining wall.

ACKNOWLEDGEMENTS

Thank you to Anna McFarlane and Nicola Santilli for your help with the writing of this book.

Thank you Liz Anelli for the beautiful illustrations, Mika Tabata for the design work and Vanessa Lanaway for the insightful proofread.

I would also like to acknowledge the following people of great achievement mentioned in this book, in alphabetical order: Sir Donald Bradman AC (1908–2001), Cathy Freeman OAM (1973–), Professor Fred Hollows AC (1929–1993), John Flynn OBE (1880–1951) and General Sir John Monash GCMG, KCB, VD (1865–1931).

ABOUT THE AUTHOR

Alison Hart lives at the foothills of the Dandenong Ranges with her daughter and lots of animals, wild and domestic. The house block is so steep, you have to go down two sets of steps to get to the front door. It's nice and quiet for writing, but also a bit distracting because the view is really good. In her spare time, Alison likes reading, watching old movies, and opening and closing the door for the cat. Besides writing, Alison works in community aged care. *School Rules are Optional* was her first novel.

Turn the page to see where
the adventure began for
Jesse and his friends ...

'Prepare yourself for a rollicking ride!' NAT AMOORE
author of *Secrets of a Schoolyard Millionaire*

THE GRADE 6 SURVIVAL GUIDE

SCHOOL RULES ARE OPTIONAL

ALISON HART

'A full-on fun fest!' OLIVER PHOMMAVANH
author of *Thai-riffic!*

OUT NOW!

The school year only started half an hour ago and I've got three problems already.

For a start, I've been put into Mrs Leeman's class. She's not even meant to be a Grade 6 teacher. I already *did* my time in Prep. I'm pretty sure she's about a hundred because she taught my dad when he was at school and he learned to write on a *blackboard*. She wears little wiry glasses and has little wrinkly eyes looking through them, hoping to catch you doing something wrong. Her hair is done up in a white bun like a grandma but she's about as far from a grandma as you can get. Everyone's scared of her. She's always yelling and hands out detentions like lollies at a Christmas party.

Secondly, there's a chance I could be a school captain this year. I was having an unusually popular day when the class voted last year. Dad had brought home a box full of irregular-shaped chocolate tree frogs from work and said I could take some to school. I took twenty-six; one for each kid in my class, and three left over. Dad does all the accounting at a warehouse packed *full* with boxes and cartons of chocolate. They have chocolate tree frogs, koalas, echidnas as well as just normal-shaped blocks and bars. They also do yucky ones with stuff like coconut, dried fruit and salt flakes.

I didn't know we were voting for school captains that day. It was an unlucky coincidence.

My third problem is that I've lost my Grade 6 jumper. The one with the year and all our names on the back. If I didn't lose it during Mrs Leeman's lecture about being responsible and looking after our stuff, I lost it soon afterwards because now I'm looking around in assembly and everyone's wearing their jumper except me.

Lastly … it's *a million degrees* today.

So that's actually *four* problems.

It's worse than I thought.

Everyone in the gym is laughing and talking about their holidays. Even the teachers.

Jun is sitting next to me with his jumper on *backwards* with the hoodie bit over his face trying to block out the sun. Jun is one of my friends. He lives with his grandparents who are really old and only have to go to work when they feel like it. Everyone likes him because he's always doing weird stuff like bringing a dehydrated lizard in a jar to school or eating seven jam rolettes for lunch.

He thinks the school rules are optional.

My best friend Alex leans over to me and says, 'Jesse – *shoes!*' and I start laughing because our principal, Mrs Overbeek, wears the same ones *every* assembly. They look like canoes made out of old rope.

Alex has been my best friend since the first day of Prep, when I accidentally squashed his finger in the toilet door, then clonked the door back into my own head. There was only one ice pack so we had to take turns. That's how easy it is to make friends in Prep.

Mrs Overbeek is standing on stage waiting for everyone to be quiet so she can get started on her boring welcome speech. She could be waiting a while. It's so hot in the gym, everyone starts taking their jumpers off. Those of us that *have* one, I mean.

Eventually Mrs Leeman stands up and the clomping of *her* shoes across the stage is enough to make the whole school turn around to face the front in total silence. She looks even more cranky than usual, if that's possible. Mrs Overbeek starts her standard first-day assembly. No one's listening though; we're all getting fidgety and uncomfortable sitting on the floor in the heat. There's no sign of our vice-principal, Mr Wilson. He probably only has to do stuff if Mrs Overbeek's not at school for some reason.

After about a year, the new kids are asked to stand up just in case they're not feeling uncomfortable enough already. There's a new girl in the other Grade 6 class. She's got the longest hair I've ever seen. It touches *the floor* when she sits down. It's not tied up or anything, so it's a good thing she's not in our class. Mrs Leeman has a no-tolerance policy when it comes to long hair not being tied up.

It's *so hot* and *so boring.*

I can't believe how hot and bored I am.

Alex hands me a sticky note with a drawing showing Mrs Overbeek in the Jurassic Period. It's a pretty good drawing. The dinosaurs are very realistic-looking. They look like they're on the brink of extinction due to heat and boredom.

He's very good at capturing the moment.

I put the drawing in my pocket. I'd like to make it through the first day of school without a detention.

Now it's *unbearable* in the gym. Mr Winsock, the sports teacher, is taking regular gulps from his water bottle – something I've noticed sports teachers do even when they're not doing anything sporty.

There's a bit of fluffing around on the stage, then Mr Wilson and a lady from the Parents' Committee come out to announce the school captains. They've probably been waiting in Mr Wilson's air-conditioned office until now. Everyone sits forwards and listens for the first time since assembly started. I'm sweating even more, and shaking. If I *am* a captain, I'll have to accept my badge from down here on the floor.

Mr Wilson takes the microphone from Mrs Overbeek and *thanks* her for the assembly so far. Then he starts talking about the *privilege* of being a school captain before *we've* had the privilege of knowing who the school captains *are*.

'And don't forget, girls and boys in Grade 6 … uhhh … while there are only two captains, it's up to *all* of you … uhhh … to set a good example for the younger students …'

I wish he would just get *on* with it.

Suddenly something goes '*crash*' over near the side door and everyone's heads swivel around.

I stretch my neck forwards to get a better look. Miss Agostino, the Prep teacher, has fallen off her chair and onto the floor.

Jun's muffled voice comes out from behind his hoodie, 'What was *that*?'

'Miss Agostino's *fainted*!' Alex says. 'She's gone like … *splatt.*'

A couple of parents who are not filming the whole thing rush forwards from the back to help Mr Winsock, who is trying to help Miss Agostino. Mrs Leeman appears on stage with a Duty Teacher vest and announces assembly is over, though Mrs Overbeek and

Mr Wilson are standing right there. She doesn't need the microphone. The Preps are led out through the canteen and given an icy pole to eat under the only shady area in the whole school until their teacher can stand unassisted. I hope they don't think it's standard procedure to get an icy pole after assembly. If they do, that'll be the first of many school-related disappointments.

While we're in the corridor, Mr Wilson's voice announces over the PA system: 'Uhhh ... yes ... hello again everyone. I'm pleased to report ... uhhh ... Miss Agostino is fine ... no need for concern. We didn't finish our assembly today, so, uhhh, we'll meet again tomorrow ...'

Jun says, 'She probably did it on *purpose*.'

'Did what on purpose?' I ask.

'*Miss Agostino*. She probably *pretended* to faint so that Mr Wilson would stop talking.'

Alex says, 'I don't think so ... you can't *make* your face go that colour.'

I run in front of the rest of the class so that I can have a quick look around the classroom for my jumper.

I look underneath my chair, on the floor, in my bag. Then I feel a chill. Mrs Leeman is miraculously back at her desk already, eyeing me from across the room.

There must be more than one of her.

I don't think she's noticed I've lost my jumper though. If she had, I would know about it.

**Find out what happens next
in *School Rules are Optional*!**